THE WIG MY FATHER WORE

Other books by Anne Enright:

What Are You Like?
The Pleasure of Eliza Lynch
The Gathering

The Wig
My Father Wore

ANNE ENRIGHT

GROVE PRESS
New York

First published by in Great Britain in 1995 by Jonathan Cape

Printed in the United States of America
Published simultaneously in Canada

Library of Congress Cataloging-in-Publication Data

Enright, Anne, 1962-
    The wig my father wore / Anne Enright.
        p. cm.
    ISBN-10: 0-8021-3832-2
    ISBN-13: 978-0-8021-3832-3
    1. Women in television broadcasting—Fiction. 2. Dublin (Ireland) —
Fiction. 3. Young women—Fiction. 4. Angels—Fiction. I.. Title.

PR6055.N73 W5 2001
823'.914—dc21   2001033520

Grove Press
an imprint of Grove/Atlantic, Inc.
841 Broadway
New York, NY 10003
Distributed by Publishers Group West
www.groveatlantic.com

07 08 09 10 11 12   10 9 8 7 6 5 4 2

FOR MARTIN

Stephen

By that time I needed anything I could get, apart from money, sex and power which were easy but hurt a lot. The angel rang at my door with an ordinary face on him and asked for a cup of tea, as was his right. He revealed himself on the threshold with broad comments about my fertility. Who needs it? I felt like taking the cup right out of his hand.

We wrestled for a while, which was just part of the job as far as he was concerned. I thought he had been wafting about since Aye began, in that place where grief and joy are one, where knowledge is an old joke and Time is just another window. I thought he might do a lot of singing. I was wrong. The angels he knew were ordinary men who killed themselves once when times were bad. Now they had to walk everywhere, setting despair to rights, growing their wings.

I said I was glad that this was the way it turned out, that I thought everyone was too hard on suicides. It isn't as if, I said, you did it just for fun. He said being an angel wasn't a free ride either. There was a lot of wrestling involved, a lot of regret. He wished, for example, that I would stop looking where his crotch kind of glittered while the rest of him glowed. He asked me how the despair was coming along. I smiled. I told him he was wasting his time on me.

Stephen had been gaffer for a construction company in Canada with some accounting duties and responsibility for a lot of materials and transport. He built a bridge in Regina and went on from there. Getting married was one of those surprises, he said, when you're just a kid yourself, but his daughters were the saving of him (they taught him how to read), and the bridges were great. Then there was all that clear sky and the crisp winters when your hand might freeze to the girders and you couldn't feel a spanner except as a burn. He was in Ontario in 1934 with a job nearly done, each side of the span cantilevered out over the water and gaping. One night he walked up to where the road stopped and stepped over to the other side. Actually, the noose froze. It was the cold that did for him in the end.

That was it, he said, and nothing left, apart from a lingering pain for humanity and a susceptibility to the weather. He gave me a smile of celestial beauty which spread over most of him, but missed the marks on his neck.

'So what's it like since God died?' I asked with a laugh. He looked at me.

'And how's your mother?' he said. Which I thought was a little low, since she is fairly happy now, considering. Besides, there are things between every mother and child best forgotten, when we all settle down and just get on with it.

Apparently this was just a stock question and second on the list. His own mother had doubled up with grief one day while clearing the dishes. She looked like she was trying to push her head into the teapot, because she had to press her face against something and she could not cry.

I was disappointed with all this mother-and-teapot lark. She was not the last thing he had thought of, before he died. I told him to get on with it and he went through the list.

THE LIST
Did my mother weep, did my father die, did the two
happen around the same time and which one caused the
other.
Did I leave lightbulbs burning alone, did I draw the
curtains at night, did I ever put a plug in a socket just to
make it feel happy.
Had I ever pissed myself in public, did I take pleasure in it.
Did I suffer from the feeling that I had left something
behind in a train. Is that why I smoked, so I could check
my pockets for cigarettes.
Had I ever been overheard in a private conversation. Had
I ever put blood on a mirror. During the sexual act did
I suffer from regret.
Did beauty disgust me.
Did Jesus Christ die for me.

Did I ever hoard parts of another person's body, for example a lock of hair.
Had I ever seen a pregnant woman swimming on her back.

I found my sexual feelings for Stephen quite disturbing. He had taken the precaution of sleeping with me at night. We were both looking for the question that was missing off the list and we needed all the time we could get.

Besides, there were problems at work. I thought about him as he lay beside me, not making a dent. Just my luck I said, cold hands and a rope burn, but he whispered in his sleep until even the sheets looked happy.

And then there was always his ineffable smile of incredible beauty. There was also the fact that he was blessed, that all the blessings ever given or withheld seemed to sit in him, for example the blessing my mother never gave me and the one I never gave her, despite the fact that we are both superstitious that way.

There was also awe and awfulness, always a good one between the sheets. Not to mention the unutterable, the unspeakable and the inexpressible, lying by my side in hand's reach.

'You're forgetting about purity, wisdom and grace,' he said. 'Even a human can have them.'

'No I'm not,' I said and made a pass at him saying 'This is pure, isn't it? This is wise?' and a lot of other very embarrassing things, as one does in these situations.

He said he thought that nymphomania was out of fashion

now, but where he came from it caused a lot of parental concern. Various procedures might be followed, with or without the aid of anaesthetic, he said, and the mildest cure of all was a bag of powdered camphor hung around the woman's neck. So he got out of the bed to look for mothballs.

We were no nearer the question as he hovered six feet over the bed and cried all night.

By breakfast time I knew what I wanted to say. I wanted to say 'It's not as if you don't think about it too, you bastard, about warming your cold hands in my hot crotch, not to mention the last thing you did, before you died.'

'I cast my bread upon the waters,' he said.

My mother rang to tell me that I wasn't at work.

'You're not at work,' she said. 'Are you all right?'

'It's Saturday,' I said. 'How are you?'

'I'm fine,' she said, because we both lie the same way. 'Any news?'

'Nothing much,' I said (there is an angel in the kitchen, breaking the toaster), 'and yourself?'

'Oh nothing new here.' (Your father is dying, but so are we all.) So we hung up.

Stephen watched the television. He sat on the sofa and laughed. When the weather forecast came on he looked at the satellite picture, said 'Wrong again! Ha ha ha.' He told me about an angel of his acquaintance who had killed himself three different ways at once. His death, when it came, was so violent, that he was still scattering and now, instead of walking, he fell like the rain.

And then there was the guy, he said, who died to the sound of sex in the next room, which was, he thought, quite a nice way to go.

'He specialises in the sound of kisses and their colour.'

'Really,' I said thinking about red.

We sat there all day, fighting over the remote control, waiting to see which one of us would snap. He cried at the news, or laughed inappropriately. I did the same at *Little House On the Prairie*. He annoyed me by pointing out an actor in the crowd.

'I know him. Cyanide. 1964. Lovely guy. Specialises in the mothers of homosexual men and shoes.'

Then there was the show I was working on. It was called the LoveQuiz. I said 'Have you ever seen anything so awful in all your life?' and Stephen said 'It's about Love, isn't it?'

So I went into work and made people love each other for a while.

The next weekend I took him into town. I was hoping he would bump into someone more needy and snag on to their grief in the crowd.

I had to hold his arm walking down the street to get him through all the pain between the GPO and O'Connell Bridge. He knelt down outside Clery's and took some dirt up off the street like a child. So I brought him inside, down to the hardware department and explained toasters to him, just to make the effort. I could tell by his enthusiasm that he missed the passage of time, he missed his body, more than he missed the body of his wife.

By the time we got to the river I loved him. He sang the Canadian Boat Song for me. The rain didn't wet him and the wind blew right through.

We looked down into the water and I said that maybe we could make a go of it after all. I would give up money if he liked, and lust, if he had to be old-fashioned. I said that there was something between us that was real and strange and just because he denied it, didn't mean that it wasn't there. The end of his nose went white. He said to me 'If dying wasn't enough, how do you think that sex would help?'

'You're just like the last man I went out with,' I said. 'At least he put out.'

He began to sing.

He was still singing when my mother called to the house with some food in a Tupperware box. They seemed to get on fine.

'No-one sang like that for me,' she said.

'If you want him, you can have him,' I said.

'Thanks for the chicken,' she said. 'It's nice to see you still care.'

'Don't be so bloody sarcastic,' I said and left them both in the kitchen, talking about God.

I went into the sitting room and turned on the television to cover the sound of their voices. For a shy woman, my mother is remarkably loud. She said 'I feel sorry for young women these days, so much is denied them.' She said 'It is a pity that she can't sing. I always thought that a singing voice was the best gift of all. Never mind all the rest.' I turned up the television and started banging my head off the wall.

'You know what I think,' she said as I showed her out, 'about you and men?'

'Yes,' I said. 'Now fuck off Ma and leave me alone.'

Stephen came into the hall. She turned to him. 'Where did I go wrong?' she said. 'The summer I was pregnant with this young woman, I swam in the sea every day, in the sun and in the rain. And I said to God that this would be my prayer for the child — whoever it was, whoever it turned out to be. And now,' she said, 'now look at her.'

That night I kicked Stephen out of the bed. When I got up to go to the toilet I found him naked, hanged by the neck in the shower. He said it helped him to think, but his small wings were a bit forlorn. By morning he was cheerful again. He announced that he had half an answer at least. It was not his place, he said, to care.

I rang my mother and told her we were not to blame.

Keeping It Wet

Keep it wet, says Frank, the director on the LoveQuiz, because he thinks we work in a whorehouse. I say Thank you Frank, but I work in a professional organisation.

OK. So I work on the LoveQuiz. Pass the barfbag. I work on the LoveQuiz. I believe in the LoveQuiz. To an extent. I get drunk and defend the LoveQuiz and I defend what people do and what we make people do on the LoveQuiz which is, after all, a matter for their own free will.

Stephen has ideas about free will, being an angel and full of shit.

The LoveQuiz is pink. It is a success. It has a cosy and dangerous host, fake games, real sex and a lot of laughs. It is a great and embarrassing show. Sometimes it is just embarrassing, but there you go, we usually get drunk on a Friday.

The office is a mess, full of the clatter-bang and howl-around of airwaves in crisis. People run around like it was a labour ward for the blind. They shout to make themselves clear, they whisper that the baby has no eyes. The phones are ringing, the vases stand empty, a male pin-up is stuck to the filing cabinet, ripped at the waist. In the corner is the hiss of an empty television, switched on, with nothing coming through. It is not simple.

On the wall is a board that says:

	Everyone (A&B)	Filming	Studio
MON	MEETING P.M.	A TRAVEL BACK A.M.	B SCRIPT MEETING
TUE	AUDITIONS A.M.	B SET UP	A SET UP
WED	DESIGN MEETING P.M.	A SHOOT I/V	B RUNNING ORDER
THUR		A EDIT	
FRI		A EDIT	B STUDIO
SAT		B TRAVEL + SHOOT	P.P. EDIT + DUB TX
SUN		B SHOOT	

NOTE: A = GRACE + JO   B = MARCUS + HELEN
ON EVEN WEEKS REVERSE A + B

Thanks for the born again Christian you bastards.
I thought we couldn't light anyone over six foot three?

10

We used to knife each other a lot but we don't bother any more. It never made any difference anyway.

Most things soak away and are forgotten. Marcus and I have forgotten that we had a carnal moment, or didn't have a carnal moment or nearly had a carnal moment back in the good old, bad old days when everyone drank too much and said too much and ended up in hospital or in Channel 4; the days when we used to stay in the office to help shove the show out on the air, like crashing a truckload of carrier pigeons. We'd get a crate of beer and shout at the food and the mud and the water and the money. Then we'd shout at each other while I stole a bottle of whiskey from the LoveWagon's office and tried to persuade either Marcus or Frank to piss in her bottom drawer, because I couldn't do it all by myself.

These days we just work together and have a bit of a laugh. The show rolls on and doesn't care. We blame the LoveWagon, because she is the boss. Not that she is ever there, but someone has to be getting something out of all of this.

The LoveWagon stands in the middle of Marcus and Frank's mezzanine. They are always running up the down-escalator towards her, or sailing past on their way to the wrong floor. They discuss her like she was a person; her clothes, her decisions, her breasts, her lies, whether she is fierce, or gentle, or real at all. Meanwhile, the escalators slow down or speed up, or change from up to down and she stands there, looking, with the phone in her hand.

I don't let her affect me one way or the other. She is a

woman. She has been up and down herself a few times. Now she is up. She drinks.

When she is drunk she talks about Television. She makes Right and Wrong sound like a body odour; something exciting, banal, something she can never quite wash away.

When she is sober she talks about danger, about keeping the show *dangerous*. She decides that the station has lost its *bottle*, that a guest doesn't *smell* right, that we are getting *drag* from the studio floor, that our presenter is *two coupons short of the toaster*. When she is drunk she says that we are *helping to build a new Ireland*.

When she is sober she says 'Great show you guys', because she believes in giving credit where Credit is due.

THE CREDITS

Researchers
Elaine Somebody
And
Production Assis....
Jo flies past
with
Floor Manager
Dear God
Cameras
Missed it
Sound
Huh?
Lighting
Hang On
Make Up
Haron By
Graphics
Oh
Vision Mixer
Location Camera
Location
Dubb
?

Producers

ah

Marcus O'Neill
Grace oops

Director
Frank

Series Producer
The Love Wagon

14

So fifteen seconds to the Opening Animation. Stand by on the floor. Coming out of this to 4 on the top shot, camera 3 on the wide, then 2 on the fat bastard. I didn't say that. VT Rolling. (Sorry I have to smoke.) Aaaaand Take It. (Tumpty tumpty tumpty tum) Standby Grams. Coming to the track on 3. GO GRAMS. And 3. And OFF you go Peter. Nice.

VOICEOVER: Ladies and Gentlemen it's . . . the LoveQuiz! And here is your LoveHost . . . DAMIEN HURLEY!

Applause applause applause. Cue Damien and 2.

STOP! STOP!

Keep going. Coming to Camera 1 on the guys.

Stop-it I-love-it-do-it-again. More More More!

Camera 3 Audience shot. Audience shot. Take it fuck him and 2.

No really. No really. MY we're all excited. We're all of a tither toNIGHT.

Back on script.

So who's going to find LOVE on the LOVEquiz this week? YOU won't believe what we've got lined up for YOU tonight. I PROMISE there won't be a dry LEG in the HOUSE.

Retake later.

And speaking of LEGS, here's this week's lovely lady. She's the gal who's going to pick the lucky fella. She's de-lovely, she's delightful MARIE from Donny-CARNEY!

Cut 4! Camera 3 give me Marie. Cue Marie Cue Marie. And 3.

Whoops. Hang on Marie. Hang on everybody. Hey! Just testing. Yes you're right! It's the FELLAS first!

Get back on 1. Cue applause. Get back. Get back. Take it. That's our edit. And 2. Suffer on.

I don't know what there is to worry about. Nothing really untoward has ever happened on the LoveQuiz despite the fact that it is all in the hands of one unknown girl. The ache of one hundred and forty planning meetings, the agony of seventy weekend shoots, the anguish of six hundred and twenty-three phone calls to Props, bunches up and halts, breathless, waiting for her word, her simple whim. 'I choose number 3.' She could have chosen 2 or 1, but statistically speaking she will choose 3, which is why we put the most attractive down that end.

No-one has ever said 'I choose number 15', for example. No-one has ever declined to choose. No man has stood up in the audience and said, 'I object, this woman is betrothed to another.' No woman has shouted 'Dyke!' No clerk-of-the-court has unfolded, solemnly or not, the birth certificate to show that she is under age. No man in a rumpled suit has walked across the studio floor, excused himself in German and pulled up her dress to show the penis underneath.

She simply says 'I choose number 3' and with music, tears and laughter, as the credits unroll their speech of modest thanks to the women who arranged such lovely flowers, she kisses and walks away with her Number Three. The studio walls give way, the plane stands ready in the scene dock, the band plays as it mounts into the sky, while an ecstatic air hostess waves and lets fall a bloodied sheet on to the camera below.

'No,' says Damien, blowing into hospitality. He's a rotund little boy, one of the great dictators. When he looks at you, you feel like you are the only person in the room, when he looks away, you despise him. We get on really well.

Frank, who was in the box directing, is twitching in the corner with a large gin and a face as blank as the breeze. They ignore each other. Instead Damien comes up to me, not because it's my show this week, but because I like him.

'No,' he says.

'No what?' I say. 'It was great.'

'No more little wankers from Dun Laoghaire.'

'He made the show.'

'I make the show.'

'Fuck off and have a drink. It was great.'

'Where were my cues?' He says he was standing there like a prick at a dykes' picnic waiting for his cue when he gets a load of custard in the face. I say that was the best bit, even though the custard hit a camera which went down. Even though those cameras cost as much as a five bedroom house on the southside, now missing a back wall. He says 'Was my reaction OK?'

So he set the custard gag up himself — anything for

attention. He knows I know, so he blames Frank. You have to hand it to him for nerve.

'No cues. Fucking snob. He cuts my best line. We had to retake the opening without my best line.'

'That wasn't Frank's decision. That was my decision. Now go over and complain to the LoveWagon. She's looking lonely.'

'Fucking right. Fucking producers.'

Ten minutes later the audience is doing a conga down the corridor and abusing the security man. Damien sits down for a brief stupor on the couch before leaping up and slapping backs like some kind of backslapping machine. The LoveWagon goes around the room and is muttered at — by Damien, by cameras, by sound, by the guy from the farting cushions company. She nods a lot, especially at Frank.

Frank is a good director. He is also my friend. Maybe this is why he lets his fingers land on my thigh like he can't remember whose leg it is.

Every week he tells me that revenge is a complicated thing, that murdering Damien would be nice, but not as effective as just putting him on screen. When he dips his head to take a drink, it's like he's probing his gin like a flower.

Marcus comes up for a fight. 'Sorry about the date package, the cameraman had diarrhoea.'

'Swings and roundabouts.'

'Here we go,' says Frank, even though I haven't opened my mouth.

Because Marcus has green eyes or brown, depending on the light. The brown eyes like me well enough, the green eyes call me a fucking animal. In the old days Marcus used to say 'I wonder about you. I wonder if you are a woman at all.' Tonight he just says:

'The custard was good.'

'Thanks.'

'What about Your Woman?' says Frank.

'Awful,' says Marcus. 'Brilliant.'

'I'm in love,' says Frank.

I say, 'I think she's in her dressing room.'

'Right.'

'I think she's having a little weep.'

At which point Marie from Donnycarney comes in, her eyes red and excited. We tell her she was wonderful and the room gives one last surge, shatters and heads for home. The LoveWagon exits like the Queen Mother, stumbling at the door. Marcus cools down. Frank falls out of love. Half an hour later the three of us are bored again, standing in the middle of the road trying to flag a taxi into town.

We split up in the nightclub. I see a man I slept with once or twice. I roar at him over the music. I say 'You think I'm a woman. You think I'm a woman. Don't you? You think I'm a woman.' So he takes me home. As we leave I can see Marie from Donnycarney trying and failing with Marcus. Her LoveDate is moping in the corner. They should both be tucked up in their beds, but I can't work all the time. I hope that Marcus will sleep with her so I can fry his ass next Monday, but I doubt it. He was never that kind.

The next day is Saturday — the morning after the night before, swimming through the show that is still swimming through me, waiting to be ambushed as I turn a corner by a little piece of dead adrenalin floating through my heart.

I am late. Jo is sitting quietly at her desk staring at the phone. The crew is at the airport waiting for Marie who is nowhere to be found.

Jo chases flights, while I chase Marie, who has not booked out of the hotel. When I arrive, her clothes are still scattered across the empty room. The phone rings. It is Jo with three near options — not near enough. We decide to go to Killarney instead. I consider calling the LoveWagon, decide against it, consider resigning, wash my face and sit down to wait.

There is a pair of shoes on the bed. There is a pair of tights abandoned on the ground. I want to switch them around. I want the shoes to be on the floor. I want the tights to be on the bed. Still, I can't touch them. They belong to someone else and they are used.

I am sweating. If Stephen were here he would pick up the tights and fold them. If Frank were here, he would put his arm around me and tell me about the sins of a married man. Marcus would ignore them, lie down on the bed and ask me what it was all about. Small mercies.

I catch the smell of last night's man. It is light and warm and I smile. I have been trying to track it down all morning.

Then I find it. It is the smell of a baby's hair. The hangover hits.

Marie walks into the room. She bends down, picks the tights off the floor, then turns to me without surprise.

'Seven pounds fifty they cost me,' she says, 'and they laddered the minute I put them on.' She sits down on the bed and switches on the television with the remote control.

'Hotel bedrooms,' she says, 'aren't they a laugh?' Oprah is on, talking to people who have been struck by lightning.

'Now I heard that somewhere,' says Oprah. 'Is that your experience? Is it your experience that when somebody is struck by lightning, that person is *thirsty* for the rest of his, or her life?'

'They'll have to do,' says Marie. 'Sorry I'm late.' And she starts putting on the tights, ladder and all.

The Wrong Place

When I come in the door, Stephen smiles hard enough to frighten a horse.

'Where were you?' he says.

'I should be in Crete,' I say.

'Where were you?'

'It's all right,' I say. 'It was just someone I know. Just someone I bump into from time to time.'

The place looks as if it died a week ago, the curtains are open to the dusk; the furniture slipping through the half-darkness. My hand sweeps past the light switch, which has drifted from its proper place. I flick it on and nothing happens. Stephen has taken the bulb out of its socket.

I walk through from room to room and my footsteps sound like they are coming from somewhere else. Every bulb is gone. The whole house is swimming, empty and electric, as the open sockets leak into the evening light.

So I sit down and try to cry and curse Stephen for it. Because we all have to get through, any way we can.

Stephen makes me a meal that is entirely white. At least it helps me see the plate. I eat by the light of the TV with the sound turned down. At the accustomed time, and by the usual miracle, the LoveQuiz flashes into the room, thin, silent and over-excited. Every time I look up, Marie from Donnycarney is watching her own legs, as if they belonged to someone else. In studio the day before, it had been a pretty randy show, but flickering on the box, lonely, with no applause, it looks vaguely obscene and inconsequential, like an old woman tap-dancing, or a dog humping a sofa during afternoon tea.

'It's on its way to God,' I say — as I always say when the credits roll. Which is how, I suppose, I got into this mess in the first place.

I fall asleep on the sofa and dream about sleep. I dream about sleep so profound and dreamless it would change everything. Perhaps Stephen wakes me in the middle of the night. He is carrying a candle. Transmission has shut down and the test card shines out into the room.

In the morning I drive to Killarney and shoot Marie.

'Pretend it's nice and hot,' I say. 'Cheer up,' I say. I tell her to push her date into the swimming pool. I tell her to show a bit of leg.

Because you can't be a snob and work on the LoveQuiz. Which means that most people on the show are in the wrong place. They feel their work as a kind of stain. I have no time for that. As far as I'm concerned, if it's not embarrassing, it's not worth it. I am intimate with the subject of shame. I am the daughter of a man who used to wear a wig. After that, I said, television is easy.

Aerial

It was a tough, wiry wig with plenty of personality. It rode around on his head like an animal. It was a vigorous brown. I was very fond of it as a child. I thought that it liked me back.

I don't know when he started to lose his hair, my mother never discussed it. Unlike her children, my mother was well brought up. As far as she was concerned, the wig might as well have grown there. I do not believe her. All children are raised on these simple lies. Your granny is in heaven. You came out of God's pocket. Daddy was always bald. Daddy was never bald.

My mother and father met in a ballroom in the Fifties, where the lights never dimmed. He was twenty-seven years old. The smell from the wig, if he was wearing the wig, would have been already high. Perhaps he kept his hat on when he asked her to dance, because men are brutish that way. Perhaps my mother saw the crippled look on his face.

What more could any woman want, than a rude, wounded man?

Those were the days when a man was allowed to be stupid. He could eat with his knife, or not wash his underwear; he could do the wrong thing to get the girl and then find that it was the right thing after all. He might be lured into the discreet back room of a hat shop as easily as he would be lured up the aisle. He did not expect his children to tug at his hair, or his wife, in the dark. Those were the days when a wig made no difference in a marriage. ('What are you looking at woman, have you never seen a bald head before?')

So they danced in the Ierne ballroom, a man with his hat on and a woman who would not let her hands stray. And they were grateful for it.

We grew up with a secret that everyone knew. Even the cat knew and stalked it. For years my father's wig felt like an answer. I could say 'I am the way I am because my father wears a wig.' I could say 'I am in love with you because I have told you, and no-one else, about my father's shameful wig.' This is not true. I have told strangers about my father's wig in discos. I have discovered that it is not a good way to score.

We lived in a house that did not believe in the past, the place where people's hair fell out. My mother kept three photographs hidden in a drawer, which we didn't need to see, in order to know. The first is a picture of my parents' wedding day. They look noble, and sweetly sad. My father is holding his little hair down in the wind. The other two were taken on their honeymoon. My mother is sitting on a rug in a bathing suit. I am already in her tummy. Then my father is on the same rug. He is standing on his head.

We do not need these pictures. My brother remembers pulling at my father's hair as a small child. He says he remembers a tuft coming away in his hand. He is still waiting to be forgiven. I remember being carried on my father's shoulders and a light sweat breaking on his scalp. My sister remembers his hairbrush, a sacred, filthy thing.

These are late memories. They came when he was sick. We thought the wig would beat us to the grave. We looked at him in his hospital bed and the dead thing on his head looked more alive than he did.

So we betrayed him. We laughed. We called it by name. 'Wig,' I said. My brother Phil said 'Toupee', because his own hair was getting thin. Brenda, the youngest, said 'Rat', which is also a word for penis.

Because the truth is that my father walked into a hair clinic in Dublin in 1967 and pushed his money over the counter, which in 1967 was a modern, Formica counter, to a woman, who in 1967 was wearing a beehive, at least half of which was fake. And in return he got a wig full of straight, stiff, dead hair, half-oriental, half-horse, that was dyed a youthful orange-brown. He had finished reproducing. I was nearing the age of reason. My mother's gratitude was wearing thin. He came home with the thing on his head. He went into work the next day. No-one said a word.

I was five at the time and in love with his forearms,

which were smooth and hairy and smelt of the sun. I knew him.

Besides, I thought the wig was part of the television set he brought home with him the same evening. I thought it was an aerial of sorts, a decoder, or an audience response.

My father still has beautiful hands, with big knuckles that his grandchildren, if he had any grandchildren, would pick up one by one and splay out on the arm of his chair. But I did not recognise the white slabs flattened against the glass when he kicked the bottom of the hall door one night, a big brown box in his arms. We stood and looked.

'Stop kicking that door!' said my mother.

'There's a man outside.' So she stepped into the hall with her own hands wet. They were cold by the time she reached the latch. The man pushed past her and set the box on the floor. It was our father. He said that there was a surprise inside, but we had to eat our tea first.

When we were called into the sitting room, a smaller, inside box was balanced on a chair in the corner by the curtains. My father (who had something strange on his head), sat us in a row on the sofa and turned the box on. Nothing happened. Then it warmed up like the radio and glowed with sound. A sheet of light fused between the glass and the thick grey of the tube. It was thinner than the film of oil on a puddle in the road and much harder. And it was dancing.

Phil asked what it was, which I thought was silly because I knew it was the television, but my father received the question solemnly, took the *RTE Guide* out of his raincoat pocket and said, '7.25: Steady as She Go-Goes with Maxi, Dick and Twink.' He walked over to his seat and assumed a viewing position.

There were people jumping around. Then you saw their faces. And there was my father, with his coat still on and his face made elastic, slight and old, by the aerial sitting on his head.

Now when my granny got her false teeth a few years later, she sat us up on her knee one by one. 'Do you want to know a secret?' she said and amazed us by pulling the teeth out an inch or two before snapping them back for a kiss. My father, on the other hand, just stopped moving his head. His neck got stiff and angry. The wig slept on top of him with one eye open, watching us. My parents' bedroom became even more secret, as if the wig were a dog at the door.

As I say, I liked the thing well enough, although I never gave it a chance. I was always one step ahead of it and my father seemed to be on my side. He was gracious and private and rarely walked down the street with us. In fact, as a family, we were quite proud of my father, of the way he held himself separate. The wig was his way of showing his anger, of being polite.

Anyway, I loved him so much that it was difficult to see him. Even now I cannot remember his laugh or his face.

It is too easy to say that my father bought the television as a decoy. I prefer to think of it as another leap of faith. Certainly, he was excited by the moon and the possibility of putting men on it. It was important that we should know about the world. And the first week of the television was also the week of the moon orbit by Apollo 8, whose pictures I did understand, because I had seen the moon and because there was no-one singing and dancing on it for no good reason, like Maxi, Dick or Twink.

My father watched the LoveQuiz once, just to be polite. He said he preferred programmes that weren't so 'set up'. I tried to tell him that all programmes are 'set up' but his wig shouted me down. I always knew the little bastard would get me in the end.

How It Was

Stephen has, by means Angelic, found a newspaper for July 19th 1969, my first night's viewing. And there it is. There is *Steady As She Go-Goes*, sandwiched between *The Doris Day Show* and *The Virginian*. It is the night of the orbit, not by Apollo 8 as I had thought, but by Apollo 11, the mission that put the first men on the moon. These tricks of memory do not distress me. I always knew that the picture of my father at the door was more miraculous than true.

Now my childhood rearranges itself, the phantom Apollo 8 is relegated to a kind of misalignment of the pixels, the shadow of another channel breaking through. Because clean as a sword coming out of a lake, one night of my life presents itself as I knew it, without static or interference. I don't know how long we already had the television, whether twenty-four hours or two years, but the night after *Steady As She Go-Goes* was the night that we landed on the moon.

Look at these windows, marvels and wonders.

T.V. TOMORROW

5.35 "TOP CAT" (cartoon)
The $1,000,000 Derby
Benny the Ball's old nag goes mad at the: sound of ambulance bells. So T.C. pretends to be a rich sheikh and runs him in the Derby with a bell on his neck. When the bell falls off they all hare around the track in a hijacked ambulance and the horse recovers his form. He's just about to win when the **commentator** says "It looks like a photo finish!" and **the horse** screeches to a halt, turns to the camera and smiles. I remember that smile, his front hoof lifted and frozen, his face saying "Who? Me?"

6.00 THE ANGELUS

6.01 SPORT

6.15 THE NEWS

6.20 RECITALS
Jaqueline du Pre, with her sister **Iris** on piano.

6.40 APOLLO 11
The Landing Craft separates from the Command Module and **Collins** gets left behind. I can't remember this without sad and spurious **2001** soundtrack. I can't remember this without **David Bowie** singing **Major Tom**.

7.10 WORD IN ACTION
Religious programme with interviews. Never mind the moon – Here's **God**.

7.25 THE LUCY SHOW
What do children laugh at?

7.55 AN NUACHT

8.00 THE ELLA FITZGERALD SHOW
Definite fake memory of this, like the way you always loved **Motown**. And one tiny flutter of a real memory, **a black face** (my first?) in three-quarter profile, with a rind of white light along her cheek. Waiting for **the moon**; a fibrillation of the heart.

9.00 APOLLO 11: Touchdown on the Moon.
Remember that first contact, so tentative and **gentle**?

9.30 THE NEWS

9.45 "YOU'LL NEVER SEE ME AGAIN"
Thriller. **Ben Gazarra** looking for his wife, with **Leo Genn** and **Brenda de Banzit**.

10.45 approx. SPORTS FINAL
Highlights of hurling and football finals, introduced by **Brendan O'Reilly**. (I know him!)

11.15 approx. LATE NEWS

Stephen's favourite show is *The Angelus*. I thought he might be a bit bored with it by now but he says that you can't get bored in eternity, he loves repeats.

As for me, I'm still trying to remember the films I wasn't allowed to stay up to watch. I never saw *You'll Never See Me Again* because I was sent to bed. Even the astronauts, I was told, had gone to sleep. I thought this was a very stupid thing to do when you had just landed on the moon.

So I will never know if Ben Gazzara found his wife, or why she was gone. Nor will I ever remember, or remember that I forgot, Leo Genn or Brenda de Banzit, despite all the trouble they went to, making up those names. I worry about Brenda de Banzit. I worry about her as she sits in her trailer getting the character right, believing in the director, having doubts about the script. I think she may have only existed for those few minutes on the night of July 20th 1969 and that I missed her. I might have dreamt that night of Brenda finally walking on the moon, but I did not.

Of course Marcus knows who Brenda de Banzit is. First off, I've got the name wrong — it is Brenda de Ban*zie*. She was a respectable type with a soft, Fifties torso who appeared in British films like *The Entertainer* and *A Kid For Two Farthings*. Marcus invents his childhood by watching old movies. He remembers films that never made it to Bum-fuck, Co. Leitrim, which is his home town. Marcus is a hero. He has five hundred back issues of the *NME* in his bedroom, just in case anyone ever gets inside the door.

I say 'Brenda de Banzie . . . She rings a bell. I think she

might have done one of the voices on *The Herbs*', and I sing 'I'm Dill the dog, I'm a dog called Dill. Although my tail I'd love to get, I've never caught it yet', stick my tongue out at the end and pant 'Ahah Ahah Ahah Ahah.'

'I have to admire you,' says Marcus, 'you make yourself up as you go along.'

'That's right.'

'How do you remember *The Herbs*?' he says. 'You didn't even have a telly until 1969.'

'We used to watch it over in the neighbours. "I'm a very friendly lion called Parsley." '

'Your mother went over to the neighbours to watch *The Riordains* on a Wednesday night. Your father went over to the neighbours to watch the GAA matches on a Saturday afternoon. You did not go over to the neighbours to watch *The Herbs*.'

'Listen,' I say, 'I was in the neighbours. They turned on the television set. *The Herbs* was on the television set. We watched *The Herbs*.'

'What age were you?'

'Five? Six?'

'Grace,' he says, 'the neighbours only had RTE. It was 1971 before even suburban Dublin, that centre and flower of modern civilisation, went multi-channel.'

'Fuck off.'

'I hate to break it to you Grace, but *The Herbs* was BBC. You saw *The Herbs* for the first time in your trendy little adolescence, on the BBC.'

'*The Herbs* was RTE.'

'*Murphy agaus a Cháirde* was RTE, *Dathaí Lacha* was RTE. Of course you're too posh for *Wanderly Wagon*. You have to invent some fucking Protestant childhood with *Bill and Ben the* fucking *Flowerpot Men*.'

'They had an aerial.'

'That's not what I'm saying.'

'There's nothing intrinsically Protestant about *Bill and Ben*,' I say. 'You don't start making chutney and knitting hot-water bottle covers just because the gardener is on his way. You don't get more channels just by singing *Nearer My God to Thee*.'

'So what's your excuse?'

Oh but Marcus knows what everyone's game is. Marcus will be revenged on the whole pack of us — because Marcus did not escape from his family like anyone else, he escaped from history. He understands his country intimately and is hurt by the fact that it does not love him back.

I say 'You just think that "urban" means "privileged" and "inauthentic", because where you come from, everyone went to Mass and lived in a cow's arse and fucked their uncle on a Saturday night, while we sat around forgetting who we really were and trying to speak proper.'

'Yes,' says Marcus, 'that's exactly what I think.'

Still, he dresses like a successful man. I imagine his body underneath it all, soft and underused. I want to sympathise with him, for all that intellectual effort. I want to sympathise with the fact that revenge will never be enough and success is a lie. I like the way he hates me, even if it is for the wrong reasons. When he says the word 'suburban' I feel arrogant and masochistic and a little bit horny. I want to open his wallet and smell it, but I am afraid it smells of shit.

Don't ever ask Marcus about his childhood, because he will tell you, because he will be right. You ask him about any day in the past, you say 'What happened to you on the 19th July 1969?' and he will say 'That was the day that someone laughed at me.' As for me, I don't even have that much — not even a lie like that to call my own.

I rang my mother and she said we were at the seaside in the summer of 1969 and weren't anywhere near a television, so when it came to the moon-landing we listened to it on the radio and looked out the window at the moon. Thanks Ma.

As for Brenda de Banzie, she thought she might be the old one with the crinkly smile and the breathing problems on Dallas. 'That's Barbara Bel Geddes,' I said. So how was she expected to remember, when they were all of them the same and half of them dead?

'And how's your young man?' she said.

'He's fine.'

'I hope you're being good to him.'

'He has painted the kitchen,' I said.

'Well there you go.'

'He has painted it white.'

'White! That's a terrible colour for a kitchen.'

'Well there you go.'

'How did you let him paint it white?'

'He has a virginity complex,' I said.

'Grainne,' she said, 'he came to the wrong house.' My mother knows how to swing a paradox. Grainne is my childhood name, if you can call children virgins. And I changed it to Grace because at school they called me Groin.

'Grace,' I said. 'Just call me Grace.'

'A nose by any other name', she said, 'would smell.'

I went into the white kitchen and cut my hand on a can of chopped tomatoes, for which my mother is to blame. There may have been a lot of blood, there was certainly a lot of tomato. Half of it hit the white wall, like someone was shot and tried to get to the light switch in the dark. I shagged the rest of it into the bolognese, blood and all.

It did not agree with Stephen. He ended up calling God on the big white telephone. 'Gawhhd!' he said. I slept well.

Stephen has never seen God. This was part of the swiz of dying. Stephen is still working his way up — as far as he is concerned I am just one more rung on Jacob's ladder. He doesn't even know what is at the top. Dread, I suspect.

I tell him he has a long way to go, choices to make. Will he be a Throne, a Power or a Prince? Will he shine red-gold or violet? The places of the seven who stand before God are already taken, so he won't be blowing a trumpet on Judgement Day, but others have fallen and more may yet fall. In the meantime he should stop getting excited by the numbers on Sesame Street and take care of his diet, because the puke of angels smells like pestilence and despair.

He blames the food. In the kitchen onions sprout through their net bags. He turns potatoes green just by looking at them. The water tastes sweeter and there are lilies in the sink. He has a way, I think, with light. There is the sound of bursting glass as herbs outgrow their jars and dough rises like an alien in the airing press. Nevertheless, his shit smells like shit and then some.

He is getting thicker. The edges are flattening out of his face and the marks on his neck have faded to a porcelain blue. In a year's time, he says, I will be naked and chubby and carrying garlands for you. I do not want a child, I tell him, let alone a cherub.

He talks to the telly all the time now, just like the rest of us. He says 'Go on, do it!' he says 'Well that's a lie for a start!' And he cries and he switches channels — I suspect without using the remote control. When I come in from work one evening the screen is blank and there is music coming out of the speakers. It looks like DeValera and Kennedy have died again and both on the same day, or the bomb has dropped silently somewhere and they are rootin' and tootlin' for the end of the world. Then a clatter of ads breaks through and I realise it is just the picture that's gone.

Sitting in the centre of the screen is a dot, like the old-fashioned nub of light that used to stick when you turned a set off. So I go over to the box to give it a good belt. Bang. The television gives a round of applause. Stephen laughs his laugh of celestial gaiety. He has painted the glass a strange and luminous black and in the centre is a small and remarkably detailed picture of the moon.

Behind the black the pictures are jumping around, agitated and blind — contained, like a couple making love in their in-laws' house or a hoe-down in a funeral parlour.

But the moon is beautiful. Even on the television the moon looks beautiful. I wonder what is so sad about it. The Sea of Serenity, The Marsh of Sleep, The Sea of Plenty like plaster coming off a wall. My father's voice telling them quietly, if my mother is right, under the huge sky and the black noise of the waves, The Alps of the Moon, The Lake of Dreams. And there they are, settled in Tranquillity, two men in a tin pot. You can see them if you look hard.

'What a lark!' I said. 'What a jape! Now scrape that off before you come up to bed.' So that I can feel like I am winning, though probably at the wrong game. The pictures are banging against the screen, the pictures are bursting out all over as Stephen turns to smile at me. His eyes still pull at some vital desire, making my innards and lights feel clotted and strung out. Even now the moist and newborn look is fading from his face. I pull the plug and go upstairs and watch the moon through the window and remember it clearly, pixel by pixel, the screen flickering, the golf ball, the flag.

Daddy-Long-Legs

'What's all this about the television anyway?' I say when he comes upstairs.

'I want to get into it.'

'Don't do it,' I say. 'They tell you to make shite and work you to the bone. Besides, that's no place for an angel.'

'It's a good place for a dead man.'

I told him that he wasn't as dead as all that. So many of the men you meet are dead. Prick at the front, wallet at the back. So what if it makes them easy to seduce? It also makes them dangerous. They give you their white blindness. So we ended up shooting the breeze, chewing the cud, talking at the ceiling into the wee small hours. I told him about one man or another, the guy who wore two condoms, the guy with twine in his pocket, the one whose underarms smelt like barbed wire. I told him about looking back. How you lose what you look at. How you turn to salt.

It is so sweet to understand at four in the morning, the

hour when the world turns over, with the bed floating away into the darkness. So I was in love again and Stephen was sad again. He was saying 'I do want to die. Just one more time. Just once for real', and I listened to him and I held him in my arms to warm him up and soothe him down. He was light and buoyant, like a soft balloon.

'My blow-up man,' I said, because nothing felt stupid in the dark, 'My wonderful inflatable angel', and Stephen was mildly, even humanly amused.

I told him that I was in love with him and that having sex was the only way to get rid of it. He disagreed, but the nostalgia for his body became so fierce that he told me about himself, before the bridge.

He met a girl in Regina when it was still a question of wearing white gloves and doing it in the hedges, because there was nowhere else to go. Not that there were a lot of hedges in Regina. So she was wearing white gloves and the sky was flat and the land was flat. They walked along the horizon because it was all horizon and where they walked the land and the sky peeled back from one another like a zip.

Stephen said that she was only a child, that the white gloves and the smell of her summer dress were like a dirty front parlour where her aunt sat knitting. The load in his trousers was as heavy and wrong as a turd on the way home from school. He felt like he was carrying a bag of something that he couldn't put down or open and when they sat under the hedge he did not know where to put his hands, never mind the rest of him, as she sat and talked about her aunt and smoothed the white of her gloves, up and down, over and over.

He wanted to marry her. He felt that she was pure and good and soiled by life. He wanted to peel and discard her, peel and discard her. He could feel her growing in the sun, there at his side. If it weren't for the gloves, she might split at the seams. Her name was Lynn.

She was talking about justice. She was saying that her life was not fair. He stretched himself out in the sun and said 'Well what did you expect?'

'Oh just the usual things,' she said and he began to despise her. Her voice was whining and small. She was swelling like a plant. He could not kiss her.

He felt the flat of his back against the ground and remembered a waltz from the week before. He looked at her white gloves, that were loose on her hands like a bad skin. They made her fingers look squat and small.

'You're too good for me,' he said — and meant it.

'What's too good? I'm not good,' she said.

She was pretty. He rolled on to his front and laid his head in her lap. She let the cloth of her white gloves stroke his hair. He said 'I'm going to go north in a while, make a lot of money.' There would be a cottage with roses at the door.

He twisted around to face the sun. The sky was hot and flat and very near. There was a piece of her dress, a bright mountain, in the corner of his eye. She lifted her arm and caught a Daddy-Long-Legs in the white bandage of her gloved hand. Raising it between his face and the sky she picked off two of its legs and then she let it go.

He remembered what his cock was for, and his mouth. He remembered that they were two people sitting under a hedge. And while they were making love, she pulled his buttocks apart with two white-gloved hands.

This was how Stephen lost his virginity, he says, not because it was his first time, but because it was a lie. She was not pretty. There would be no cottage and no roses.

I said men are so squeamish when it comes to matters of the heart. They worry about sincerity. They think Sincerity is the last little town on the railroad track, with a freshly painted sign.

There was nothing for it but to fall asleep. I dreamed that Stephen was hovering as usual over the bed and that his tears were penetrating me, in the way of dreamlike penetrations, and that it was rape in the way that rape is not a shock but an erosion, in the way that it makes you feel older than the mountains and worn down, or so a woman told me once.

In the morning I find his tears of celestial sadness have left a spattering of faint brown marks on the sheet. I said 'What has happened to your tears Stephen? They used to be better than Ariel. They used to be liquid light.'

Love

It seems to be a cause for celebration. We have done one
hundred and fifty of the fuckers and are obliged to eat
dinner and consume wine, which isn't so bad now that we
are grown up. We have a dispensation from the LoveWagon
to like each other, without her paranoia getting in the way.
Apart from which she knows her limits, drinks herself into
silence and not into speeches about how we couldn't have
done it without Gary in Sound.

I sit beside Jo who has an instinct for order, and across
from Marcus and Frank because you need a good fight
when things start to get sentimental.

Frank says we've never had a virgin on the show, that he
can smell one from five hundred paces.

'What about Marie from Donnycarney,' I say with one
eye checking Marcus, 'convent bred, the flower of Irish
womanhood?'

'Not a chance,' says Frank. 'Convent girls go like bunnies.'

Frank likes little girls, but he is too sophisticated to like virgins. Frank wants a little girl that knows all the tricks. He's like most men I know, except he's not afraid to admit it.

'I never was a virgin,' I say. Which Frank ignores because he is perfectly sane. Frank has worked for his sanity. He has a wife and a house and he talks too much. He used to tell me how Sheilagh won't have sex at home anymore but drags him into the bathroom by the belt every time they have dinner with friends. Now he is talking about younger ass. I don't want to know. Married people should not tell tales. Being miserable in silence is the price they pay for being happy. They bought it. I did not. I am stuck with a couple of one-night-stands and an angel in the kitchen who breaks my appliances and won't put out. I understand the difference between sex and love, between love and the rest of your life. So don't let any married man tell me that he has problems with his dick. And keep their wives away from me too, at parties.

'An angel?' says Jo.

'Never mind,' I say.

'Hang on,' says Marcus. 'We were all virgins. Even you had a childhood and lost it. Or maybe you're born with a diaphragm installed, here in Dublin 4', and a little trail of insult crosses behind his eyes, like beads on a miserable string.

★　★

My mother thinks that the loss of my virginity caused my father's stroke and so do I. Never mind the facts. The first fact, fuck it, is that I never was a virgin, never had a hymen, never knew the difference between loss and gain.

The other fact is that I stayed out all night, the night my father's brain sprung a leak, and that rage kept my mother awake and in the kitchen while my father lost half of his bladder and half of his bowels into his half of the bed.

Never mind that I had spent the night talking and fully dressed, while my mother sat up, listening to the hall door opening, over and over, in her head.

So my virginity, if I ever had a virginity, was just an idea my parents had. But it was my father who took the brunt of it, because it was his brain that tore and bled and was transformed. No wonder my mother felt like a hypocrite. No wonder I felt bad.

I came in at seven in the morning to an empty house. I rang the neighbours and so broadcast the facts that I was a slut and that my father was in hospital, both at the same time. Since then, my father's illness has not been made my concern.

A few weeks later I did sleep with Brendan (large, rooted and sincere) for the first time. I mourned all right, but not for my virginity. I mourned for my mother in the kitchen and my father in the bed. I was astonished by sex. And I was astonished by the fact that the rhythm of love, when it happened, was the awful swing of my mother's hall door, always opening, never shut.

Brendan took it all very badly. We lay there in his dirty and tangled sheets. I said 'That was my first time.' I said 'My father's just had a stroke.'

'Anyway,' says Frank, 'she can't be a virgin. Not after Marcus gave her one that Friday night.'

'It doesn't matter', says Marcus, who has an urgent mind and very little in his pants, 'whether she was a virgin or not — because on the screen, for the duration of the show, for the punters at home, that young woman was *as good as a virgin*. And *that* is the lie we get paid to tell.'

'She was as good as a ride,' says Frank.

'Whore,' I said into my dinner.

'All things to all men!' said Marcus. 'Which is why, when people criticise the programme — yes, it's a trashy show, yes, it's complicated — it's as trashy and simple and complicated as a one-night-stand is, or as paying for a blow job is, or as falling in love. So when people criticise that experience, whatever it was that *they saw* on the screen, they are telling you more about themselves than they are about the show.'

'Gosh!' said Frank.

'I know what I'm looking at,' said Jo.

'Exactly,' said Marcus. 'Just what I said.'

Marcus always wins a) because he changes his mind all the time, which he is allowed to do because b) he read somewhere that truth is just a matter of building contradictions. So now he has his cake, he eats it and his shit comes out wedge-shaped with icing on the top.

'Marcus,' I said. 'I was not calling Marie Keogh a whore, whether or not you slept with her. I don't know how to break it to you, but she is just a distracted young woman we put on the telly the other night. I was calling you a whore. I could have called Frank a whore, but we all know that he'd get up on the crack of Dawn, so it's not exactly hot news. I was calling you a whore because you *get off* on television and you love talking shite.'

'And you are working for Mother Teresa,' said Marcus. 'As we well know.'

'I know what I am,' I said. 'I know that I'm out on the streets with my high heels on, earning a crust. You just hang around because you love the smell of cock.'

'Why do you *talk* like that?' said Marcus.

'I'm just talking. You're the one who is waving it around.'

'Oh. You think I slept with her.'

'I think you don't know the difference between fucking her on-screen and off.'

'And what exactly *is* the difference?' said Marcus, who wants to make Drama and doesn't put out.

'Are those shoes new?' said Frank.

He has just retrieved a fork from the floor. He ducks down again, followed by Marcus and Jo, their elbows cresting the air like whales going under, with the coffee cups sailing by. It was my shoes they were looking at, so I joined them.

Under the table the world was huge. The sounds were old. Our childhoods were sitting there, with a finger to their lips.

We looked at each others' faces, small beside our thighs, which were broad and easy on the flat of the chairs, sitting any way, privately akimbo. There were our legs, frank and tender without their torsos, thinking about the possibilities of mix and match. They might for example, walk off in different couples, leaving our bollocks and bits abandoned mid-air.

We laughed. I lifted my flanks to make them look thinner, then dropped them again and twisted my head back up, leaving them to talk in the secret way that legs might have. As I came to the lip I lost Marcus's and Frank's knees and crotches, and found their shoulders, shifting blindly along the line of the table top.

Back in the open, the sounds of the restaurant collided like two trains slamming past each other. I was still laughing. Marcus, Frank and Jo surfaced and smiled.

I knew that the trains had crashed and we had all died. It was just that no-one had noticed yet.

'These old things?' I said. 'I've had them for years.'

'Nice,' said Jo.

'Well I've met him,' said Frank.

'Met who?'

'Your man. Stephen. Met him in the bookies.'

'He is not my man.'

'Don't look at me,' said Marcus. 'I don't care.'

'Gave me a winner for the Gold Cup so I bought him a drink. And it so happens he knows my name from the credits. "Frank Fingal!" he says, "from the LoveQuiz?" "Is this fame at last?" I ask. "No," he says, "I've just moved in with Grace." '

'He's a flatmate.'

'Who's for coffee?' said Marcus.

'You shut up,' says Frank. 'All right he's a flatmate. I didn't mean to annoy you, Grace. I just . . .'

'I'm not upset.'

'I know you're not. I just wanted to say. And what the fuck do I know about women?'

'I'm not a "woman".'

'Two coffees?' said Marcus.

'Grace,' said Frank. 'Go for it. I'm serious. He's the one. OK, say you were casting something — he's the one that would jump straight bang through the lens and land in your fucking lap. And he's lucky. He's *lucky*.'

'What is going on around here?' said Marcus. This is not the Frank we know and love.

'Frank's lost the run of himself,' I said. 'He's probably doing it for a bet.'

'Oh fuck you,' said Frank. 'Fuck you, Grace darling.'

'Who's this?' said the LoveWagon calling down the table, right on cue. Which is when I realise that whatever is going on, it is not mine.

'Just a guy who asked me for an audition,' said Frank.

'Well bring him in.'

'What?' I said. 'No. No, he's wrong. He's too . . . he's too natural.'

'Natural?' said Marcus. 'What's natural? Yellowstone Park is natural. But if you throw a packet of Daz down Old Faithful it'll shoot just for you.'

'Well God knows we need a bit of right,' she said, 'after

last week. Two anoraks, a psycho and a spoilt priest. Any more shows like that and we'll be eating the cabin boy.'

'Shouldn't we pull straws?' said Frank.

'Why don't we pull contracts instead,' said the Love-Wagon with a smile, 'and see who's got the shortest?'

'Jesus,' said Marcus under his breath. 'Man the lifeboats.'

'Jump don't fall,' said Frank.

'Jump don't fall,' said Jo.

'How can you tell?' said Marcus. 'How can you tell if you're falling?'

★ ★

My father's stroke changed nothing. He still said there was no difference between blue and green. He dried the dishes and still put them back in the wrong place. He was the same, inappropriate man, except that now he was waiting for the real thing to come and tap him on the shoulder with 'COME ON SWEETHEART. TIME-TO-DIE TIME.'

So his second stroke when it came, was a strange relief. Now he lives on the wrong side of the mirror and says table instead of chair. He is not surprised and neither are we. Perhaps he wants to sit on the table after all and eat his dinner off the chair.

His death might have relieved us more. We are a very private family. We would have buried his wig with him and gone our separate ways.

My mother put a bed downstairs and took him out of

hospital because she wanted him to die in the right place. We were called back for the wait, all grown up. The ceilings were too low, the toilet was surprisingly near the ground. We slept in our old rooms, Phil shedding his own hair on to his childhood pillow, myself and Brenda polite as strangers in twin beds.

He was to die in the living room, so we turned on the telly to tease out his poor tangled synapses. We took turns at his side and waited for the peculiar silence after his last breath. I sat there thinking, Just keep going, just keep going until I'm out of the room. Da was unconscious. His fingers were swollen. Half his face was already dead. There was an Australian soap playing. I heard his last breath and I heard the silence. Then another last breath, another silence. He went on for days. We drank a lot of sherry.

I looked at his face, that I still could not remember from one moment to the next. The wig was obscenely young and jaunty on the top of his withered head. It was fake like a hero. I sat there and looked at it, as it looked back at me, and we both hung on.

The house was full of women, delighted, in for the kill. They said decades of the rosary in the front room so we couldn't throw them out. My father gave off a sweet smelling hiss of disapproval and tried to turn his face to the wall.

He managed to tell us that he was still alive:

He started to say the word Canal.

He tore up an atlas and ate all the maps of America.

We took the hint and started to fight like family again. My

mother stood by the sink and called Brenda a slut. Brenda shouted back. She said why did she always have to start an argument when she was on the toilet. She said that if she was a slut then she wasn't the only one — meaning me I suppose, though now I have the excuse of a good job. Brenda works with children. My mother thinks this is the wrong place to find a good man.

Brenda's promiscuity is the great family joke. No-one has the heart to say that she sleeps with women, least of all Brenda. She may sleep with a lot of women but I doubt it. My mother probably hopes that she has the sense to avoid housewives on benefit and go for professional women instead. Brenda's sex life, however, is entirely political. I think that she likes men well enough, she's just terrified their hair will come away in her hand.

No-one cares who Phil sleeps with. When my father dies Phil will marry a small expensive woman who knows quite a few fun people. She will be very nice and we will despise her. Phil is normal, which, as every sister knows, means buck mad. We remember him at thirteen — his horror of menstruation, his obsession with soaps shaped like animals, his religious inclinations, the delicate way he would carry an egg in his mouth after confession, as a private penance.

My mother loves Phil like a son and loves all his weaknesses, but she loves Brenda like she loves herself — the middle one, the one who is left out. They fight about everything and cry in separate rooms. They mooch around the kitchen finding things to do. As for me, I couldn't be bothered picking up a cloth to dry a cup.

I am my father's daughter. Nevertheless, when he tied his wedding ring to the cord of the lamp and plugged it in, it was time to leave home one more time.

★   ★

I only hate the LoveWagon before eleven o'clock in the morning. After noon I am quite indifferent. Late at night I find myself getting sentimental about her washed little blue eyes with the hurt sitting behind them like a stupid child.

She is doing her imitation of a woman at a party, telling stories about the days when she was out on the road. Duck and cover, wait to be seduced. 'Please like me,' she says, and it makes you feel a little soiled, a little eager. 'OK,' you say.

She tells us about the movie star with the hair transplant, the priest with his pockets sewn up, the minister for health who took the sound man aside and asked him what a blow job was.

'She *is* a woman,' says Marcus, 'she flirts like a woman.' Because as far as he knows, the only place a woman can betray you is in your bed.

Marcus is convinced that she is having an affair. He says that she has to be, that the show would have been pulled long ago if it weren't for the smell off her of someone big. Like who? I say. Like when? She couldn't be that stupid. 'But she's not clever,' he says.

She has him well fooled. Marcus thinks that someday his

talent will shine through, that he will tell them all what power is and what is television. I say he'd do a lot better to be a little thicker, which, being from the country, you'd think he'd understand. It will be a long time before Marcus gets there. He doesn't have the nose for it — or at least, he has a nose all right but his brain gets in the way.

'There is only one way to beat her,' I say. 'You can confuse her with her own stink.'

'How do you do that?' he says.

'How should I know?' I say. And he looks at me like I have two heads.

The LoveWagon is telling the story of a woman in Belfast who picked up bits of her husband out of her own front garden. It was a brilliant interview, even the sofa was right. There was a silence after the woman finished, the tears still running down her face and the LoveWagon made the slight move that is the sign to quit, a kind of undertaker's nod to the gravediggers. When the cameraman, who shall remain nameless, spoke directly to the woman and said 'I am sorry. I have a technical problem with that. Would you mind saying it again' and horror stalked the semi-d.

They did the whole lot again and it was dreadful, un-usable. And when she viewed the tape later, she saw that the cameraman had just flicked the off button! Which was the kind of thing you could get fired for, but not as bad as the way he took the woman's hand on the doorstep and looked bang into her eyes.

'I think it was sexual,' she says, 'not to mention sackable. But what can you do?'

'Maybe it was love,' says Jo.

'Love?' says Marcus.

'LOVE!' says Jo and bangs the table with her fork. We all look at her, trying to imagine the kind of love she is talking about. Love that makes you want to turn the camera off.

★ ★

I have been in love. After we all settled down, between the two strokes.

I left home. At the time I thought that it was nothing to do with my father. I thought it was a political thing, because a girl has to grow up any way she can. So I went to England, a country where women didn't bury their babies in silage pits, a country where people knew the virtues of stripped pine. Exile was mainly a question of contraception and nice wallpaper.

I woke up six months later with the feeling of a hand choking me in the dark. There was no-one in the room. I was in Stoke Newington and very little of it made any sense. If I hadn't fallen in love with an Englishman I might have gone home.

Love. Amid all that alien corn. It seemed like I had been practising for so long and still I wasn't ready; for the way the chair sat so well by the window, for paint that was too bright, for skin. He was blond. He was old enough to know better. He was restrained. There is nothing like taking the clothes off a restrained man.

It wasn't easy, this difference between one and two. I

ended up thinking about death all the time because it was simpler, his death, my death, his funeral, my funeral, the coldness of his face and my swooning to the organ in a blindness of grief.

His face was cold anyway, his eyes nice and cold and blue and his hands were both hot and soft. He used to run a bath after we had made love and lie in it and talk to me, while I sat on the toilet seat and watched the wonder of his mickey floating free. His face would be blood red in the steam, his mouth thin and pale, the roots of his hair almost white where it was stitched into the blush of his scalp and his eyes impossibly blue.

I have always found liars both subtle and exciting, for which, of course, my father is to blame. At the same time, I thought his wig was a talisman against other, less interesting lies. I thought I was immune. And yet, here I was, in Stoke Newington, watching a man wash my smell away.

I came home to the country where you could tell if a man was married, and if you couldn't, then you could always find out. Not that I could care less, because I was in love, whatever that meant, with a man who rang one Saturday morning and asked me to have his child. Certainly, I said. In Ireland we have babies just like that. We have them all the time. So I got on a plane and flew across the Irish Sea to a hotel bedroom where I took off my clothes and lay down on a candlewick bedspread and crooked my knees, and said 'I love you' and he said 'I love you' and swung his slow bollocks down to me, full of the miracle of creation.

Oh I wanted him all right; his troubled heart, his ribs like knives, his eyelids leaking a flash of blue. I wanted him so much I thought it would never happen, never end, this love you could hear, like a song in the room. So I was quite surprised to find that my body had deserted me in its finest hour, that it had slammed the door and pissed off home. What had been a space was now a rope, twisted through my guts and moored to my heart, which would not let it go. I was spitting out even the thought of him — so hard I was afraid I might turn inside out, there on the candlewick bedspread, in a little corner of a foreign hotel that was forever Ireland.

So after this dry birth, my cells taught me how to forget him, one day at a time, and my eyes would not cry for me and my womb remained tactful and serene. 'Bitch,' I said, and gave up politics with the memory of his voice and of his absolute and irreducible rightness, that didn't really need me.

★   ★

Frank has gone quiet. No jokes Frank? No jokes.

So we talk about the movies we are going to make. Marcus is going to make a comedy about Northern Ireland, because that is the only real way to approach it or a fake snuff movie with one real bit left in, just to get back at the snobs. I'm going to make a Country and Irish thriller that is about love. Love? 'A gay country and western road movie. Set in Kinnegad.'

'Not a lot of gay in Kinnegad.'

'Not a lot of road in Kinnegad.'

'You'd be surprised. So it starts with a body in the boot of a car.'

'Love?' says Frank.

'If you insist. It starts with a body in the boot of the car. Credits. No, flashback. This country and western singer he picks up a young fella in a bar, a gurrier, ordinary looking, dangerous. Loads of sex. Insane sex. And he sets him up in his flat in Dublin, with the white piano and the white ten-gallon hat, and the white bedroom with the shag carpet, and one day he comes home, comes home hot and worried and kind of poignant and horny, and there's a body on the bed. Not just any body, a dead body. So he sits on the bed, doesn't move. And then he reaches over, undoes the dead guy's shoelace, while the young fella sits in the next room and picks out a tune on the white piano.'

'Stand by your man.'

'Cut to the road. White Beamer. No, a red Thunderbird. No, it has to be white, and they're driving along with a song on the radio.'

'Stand by your man.'

'So cut to the back of the car, and there's something dripping out of the boot. There's blood dripping out of the boot, because the body is in the boot, and it is bleeding in the boot.'

'And?'

'And they have this body in the boot.'

'And?'

'Well they don't know what to do. They're just driving along, music on the radio. The boot is leaking.'

'Come on,' says Marcus.

'Well you tell me,' I say. And I mean it.

'OK,' says Marcus. 'They stop for lunch.'

'They stop for *lunch?*'

'It's a movie. They stop for lunch.'

'No!'

'Yes,' says Marcus. 'They stop for lunch. In one of these hotels on the main street that's just a house smelling of cabbage and a broken down woman serving dinner who looks like his mother.'

'And outside', I say, 'the blood is still dripping out of the boot. Dripping on to a styrofoam cup in the gutter.'

We think about this for a while.

'A young girl,' says Frank, 'the waitress, with her hair not washed, kind of . . . underused and country-sexy . . .'

'Don't tell me. A young girl.'

'No really. She arrives with the chips and she *recognises* the singer. She looks at him, and he looks at her and *she knows.*'

We stop. Too many things are wrong. So Marcus says 'He runs out through the door.'

'Yes,' says Frank, 'and when he looks back through the window, the psycho is still in there, peeling notes off his wad, like a cowboy, having a joke with the girl. Only it's the dead man's money.'

'I don't know about this,' I say.

'Whatever,' says Frank. 'The car roars off low angle and

we see the styrofoam cup in the gutter. Cut to the girl waving tragic pathetic and then she looks down and sees the cup.'

'And?'

'It's not my movie.'

'Oh come on Frank,' I say. 'There's a body in the boot of this car.'

'The girl sees the cup.'

'So they're driving along the road,' says Marcus. 'And something stops them. They get stuck in a herd of cows. All right?'

'No, not all right,' says Frank.

'Seriously, the cows smell the blood and panic. And they're climbing on to the bonnet and there's a dog barking at the boot. And there's a farmer.'

'I don't know,' says Frank.

'The psycho loses it,' says Marcus, 'and reverses over the dog? Yes?'

'No!' says Frank. 'The girl sees the cup.'

Which is when we realise. Frank has fallen in love. How can he put an end on things?

'I interviewed a man once', says Marcus, 'who nearly drowned under a herd of cows. They stampeded off the back end of a ferry.'

But Frank is in love and will have none of it. Marcus looks at me over the top of the table. This is serious. Who is it? He always got away with it before.

Because Frank likes women. He likes their hair and their hands and the fact that they are more interesting than men, when they talk. He likes the way they tell him to fuck *off*. He likes their breasts when they are young and their jewellery when they age. He is happy to find them complicated, or even false-hearted. So women like Frank. They like him in bed because he delays penetration in the recommended way, though for some this is too long and too late. Then of course, there is always his wife.

But Frank was careful. He always said that women's bodies are treacherous, and full of holes. When you can't put it off any longer they take you in and hold you, so when you flup your dick back out on the sheet, you have left yourself and all of you inside. In there. I told him that a woman's body provokes a lot more anxiety if you happen to have one yourself. He didn't believe me. Now everything is upside-down, all his careful sanity.

★   ★

My father claimed to know the secret of happiness. He said that we're better off without it. How would he know? There is only a scrap of him left in the room, the rest of him is dead or elsewhere.

The piece of my father that sits downstairs is cunning as hell. His working eye is hooded and his dead eye is fierce. He knows how to survive, knows all about revenge. He says 'The teacher who twisted my ear is dead and my ear is dead.' He says 'I bought this house for twenty-five years. The banker is dead and the money withered and the house is half dead and so am I. But only half.'

My mother too has her little ferocities. She makes him

cups of tea, she leaves the television on full blast. Sometimes she catches him trying to poke at the buttons with his stick. She takes the stick away from him and says, 'If you crack that tube, the whole thing will explode.'

It would be wrong to say that my mother does not love my father. It is with love and patience that she tends to his wig. She might have thrown it out long ago, but instead she pinched up her face, put on her rubber gloves, plucked it free and flung it in the washing machine. I like to think of it spinning around with her knickers and her bras like a rat on holiday, but my mother is much too nice for that. The wig was washed alone. She put disinfectant in the prewash to kill it stone dead. The main wash was both concentrated and biological and she put hair conditioner instead of fabric softener in the rinse, because she is thoughtful and good.

The wig went out on the line where it soaked up the smell of the sun and tortured the cat. By the end of the day it was a new thing. It had, it was true, shrunk slightly, but then, fortunately, so had my father's head.

Now she dresses the wig in the morning with her back to my father's skull. She uses a bristle brush and vigorous strokes, then she turns and crowns him, with one light gesture. She gives the wig a tug at the back and a double, symmetrical tug at the sides. It is done in silence. They both look elsewhere; though sometimes my father cannot shift his dead eye away from her. She never says the forbidden words (bald, cradle cap, wig). At their age it must be better than sex.

All the same, I fight with my mother. Upstairs, like an open window, she has hung the three secret photographs of my father in his own hair: the picture of their wedding day; the picture of my mother on their honeymoon, sitting on a rug with me in her belly; and the picture of my father on the same rug, standing on his head. It is a pornographic display.

My father is not able to climb the stairs, so he will never see the three bald photographs hanging on the wall. My mother thinks she hung them out of sight because she loves him. She says she wants to remember things as they really were. As if she didn't know, that seeing things as they really were is the greatest possible revenge.

My mother sits on a rug. My father stands on his head. His genitals are quietly upside-down, having a good time with gravity. Nothing sums up love better for me, its weight and weightlessness, its tender and inverted freefall, than the picture of my Da giving his bollocks a rest, on a Foxford rug, in the sunshine, in the first hours of my life.

★ ★

Marcus is dug into a conversation with Jo about how wonderful she is. Keep digging, says her face. It will all be one in the morning.

Frank has taken off his wedding ring and put it in his mouth. He flips it out and holds it like a monocle between his bottom lip and the base of his nose. Then he flips it back in again, holds it between his lips and teeth and sticks his tongue out through it. Is he drunk? I don't want to watch. I don't want to see the wet and remarkable red of his tongue. I don't want to see how it fills the gold of the ring. I am afraid that he will swallow the ring, that it will lodge in his gullet or in the sphincter at the top of his stomach, or in his pyloric sphincter or in, God knows, any other sphincter I could name.

Never mind Frank, I think I'm drunk myself. I imagine his alimentary tract lined and jointed with gold rings, like the neck of a Masai woman, only on the inside.

I say 'Take that out of your mouth before you choke on it', and Frank laughs like this is a really good joke. Love does not suit men.

I say, 'So will it pass?'

'Not this time,' says Frank.

'Shit Frank. You fucking eejit. Just hang on. Just hang on and keep your mouth shut and you'll be fine.' Frank laughs again.

'She knows,' he says. 'I told her last week.'

'Well take it back. Don't do it Frank. Don't even think about doing it. Don't break my heart.' I sound sincere. I must be drunk. I am drunk.

So I cannot claim to remember all the revelations that followed after Frank laughed too much and hedged a bit and drank some more and finally blurted that he has fallen stupidly, horribly, in love with his own wife. And she doesn't want to know. Why should she, fifteen years on?

I do remember the appalling detail of her childbirth scar, like an impossibly beautiful child whose harelip makes you love it, because it has a flaw.

'Of course you love your wife, you pillock,' I said, feeling abused.

'You love your wife like a wife,' he said. 'You don't love her like a fucking car crash.'

Frank was worried he might have a cardiac arrest. He got a hard-on half a mile from the house, and if he didn't plan it right he would still have it leaving for work the next morning. If he kissed her too fast when she said 'Is that you?' if he pulled her gently by the hips, with the flat of his hands wrapped around the bone and his fingers pressed into the dent on the north side of her iliac crests. If he did this at the wrong time, when she was at the cooker with a pot in her hand for example or talking on the phone, or wiping a child's nose, or any of the hundred moments where she forgot herself, and he wanted to love her into further loss, when he wanted to worry the nub of her cervix like a boy playing with the knot at the base of a balloon. If he mistook or mistimed and she pushed him away, like a wife might, instead of like the woman he loved so hard it hurt.

'Well that must be nice,' I said. 'After all these years.' Fuck you Frank.

'I can't touch her,' he said. 'She thinks I've picked up some nineteen-year-old and the guilt is making me horny. She went through my dirty shirts with a nose like a Hoover and then smashed up the kitchen because there was nothing there to smell. She says this is the last time. She says she's looking for someplace else to go', which is the funniest thing I've heard in a long time, so I laugh until I feel good.

Frank smiles. He is in love, and ordinary things are unbearable, changed and sweet. Even I am beautiful, here on the other side of the table — though who can say if it is really me. Frank's eyes make me sad for Stephen and then the penny drops.

'How long has this been going on?'

'I don't know. Forever. A couple of weeks.'

'After you went to the bookies?'

'I'm always going to the bookies.'

'After the Gold Cup?'

'How did you guess?'

'Oh just men,' I lied. 'How everything changes when they feel they're winning.'

On the other side, Marcus is telling Jo how much he would like to be in love with her. Jo's face is smiling. She knows it's just his way of complimenting people and insulting them at the same time.

'You're real,' he is saying. 'You're the real thing. You're everything I admire.'

'Well fall for me so,' says Jo. 'I don't mind.'

'I admire you too much,' says Marcus.

Down the table even the LoveWagon is getting misty-eyed, she is playing with the knife in her hand like each man kills the thing he loves.

'The thing about you is, you're not ambitious,' says Marcus to Jo. 'Even though you're better than the rest of us all put together. You put up with a load of wankers. You hold the gig together, and you never complain.'

'That's my job,' says Jo.

The LoveWagon is touching the lip of her glass with the knife. If I don't start a fight, she'll start a speech.

'Why are we talking about work?' says Jo.

'I was talking about you,' says Marcus.

'Oh?'

'I was saying how great you are, but you don't want to hear.'

'Right.'

'You're too calm, Jo. It's more than you're paid for.'

'Looks like I'm into overtime so,' she says and looks at her watch.

'Don't worry Jo,' I say loudly. 'Marcus never falls for real, even when he wants to. Marcus falls for expensive-looking women that make him think he's in the movies.'

'You know fuck all,' said Marcus.

'Then he tells them they're not real enough. He has a poor man's heart.'

'At least I have one.'

'Yeah yeah.'

'Don't you two start,' says Jo. 'Or I will lose it.'

I look at him and he looks at me and both of us wish that we could stop using the wrong organs, heart and mouth, both of them liars and nothing more appropriate down Mexico way. Poor Marcus, says the drink, poor Grace. No love lost, no love to lose — two of a kind. Which is why I say, 'You think. You think . . . well fuck you.'

★　★

My father worked for the electricity supply board. He put on his hat and walked out the door and switched the nation on. He put up pylons single handed, knotted the cables, flung them over the country like a net. He set the turbines spinning, saved old ladies from the dark. Everyone's father is a hero. Everyone's father is loved. They have it easy, in a way.

But my father did not have it easy. This is a man who had to teach his children how to swim, without getting his head wet. This was a man who could not suffer a breeze, but put us on our bikes and let the saddles go, each at the right time. This was a man who could not bear history, but bought a television set so we could look at the moon.

My father treated facts like sweets in his pocket that he could take out, surprised that there was one left. He took a personal interest in low wattage bulbs. Traffic lights made him sentimental. His children broke his heart just to look at them.

There are many other fathers I could have had. I could have had a bus-kicker for a father, who walked along the street, said 'Gyoarraughhdah' to the double-deckers, who got on at the corner and fought his way off before the next lights. I could have had a soldier for a father, who gave me fifty pence to shine his buttons and told me that men are animals. I could have had Marcus's father, coming up the stairs in his long-johns, with the soft rain streaming down and the mastitis on the heifer in the haggart. I could have had the LoveWagon's father, a cut-glass drunk, nearly a Protestant, who came home from the hospital on a Thursday evening, rattled his paper and said 'I should get a job in England. You can say what you like about English women, but they know how to wash.'

Instead I had a suburban father, an ordinary man, who bought his new house for his new children and built a better life. Why should I blame him, that he kept a little over for himself?

★   ★

Jo bangs on the table with her fork again. She hits her own chin by accident and doesn't seem to notice. Apart from that she looks entirely sober.

Marcus says, 'You're the one who should be calling the shots Jo.'

'I don't want to call the shots.'

'You should want to call the shots. You're better than her. You're better than . . .' The LoveWagon has laid her knife on the table. She looks ready. When Jo pushes her plate away like a bad memory, she takes it as a signal to stand.

'Why should I want?' says Jo.

'Don't do it!' shouts Frank and the LoveWagon smiles.

'Because you're good, that's why. You're real.'

'What's real?' says Jo. 'I couldn't be bothered.'

'Look at you. You're bothered.'

'Don't do it!' shouts Frank and the LoveWagon raises her glass.

'You're clever. You're in touch. You are the country at large.'

'You don't know the fuck who I am,' says Jo, swatting him away. 'The nearest I ever came to being the country at large was getting raped by a rich bastard. Him and the tax man. A barrister. Now there's a thing. He'd never heard of consent. Forget it. I like my job.'

Jo is limping through the silence that has fallen for the LoveWagon's speech. When she looks up twelve different monologues break out at once.

'I like my job,' she says as Marcus says 'You like your job' as I say 'Anyone want the rest of this pecan pie?' as Frank says 'The golden table' as the LoveWagon says 'One hundred and fifty. Hey! What more can I say?' and sits back down. And from the other end of the table comes Gary's voice singing, 'My young love said to me "My mother won't mind. And my father won't slight you, for your lack of kind" ' and we all relax. Now Jo can be our own again because when it comes to singing she has the voice of an angel.

The songs were as follows

Frank (badly): I am stretched on your grave.
Marcus (bravura): Raglan Road.
Everyone: Carrickfergus.
The LoveWagon: not asked.
Damien (on spoons): New York, New York.
Me (tortured recitative): The Old Triangle.

Jo (in a voice of sweet despair): When Other Lips
   (by special request): Drink to me only with thine
   eyes.

By which time everyone was pretty well on and we sat
in the rising tide of friendship like milk was slowly filling
the room while we sat up to our oxters in it, not knowing
if the gathering clots were inside us or outside but only
knowing that they were to hand. Feeling them and teasing
them out, while our eyes sentimentally left one object for
another, as if they all made too much sense.

The milk was up to the lip — its meniscus dragging out
of the wooden edge, pulling at the island the table has made
in this embarrassing, waist-high sea. Frank talked about
the Golden Circle of Someplace where the Marquis and the
Marquise, the Monseigneur and his niece, the General and
his suave subaltern, made adroit puns and political
manoeuvres and bet their estates on keeping a straight face
while men and women, under the table, unnamed and all
hungry, earned a shilling by eating their way, delicately,
respectfully, wittily, through the assembled guests — ate
moreover with their unwashed fingers and their sharp little
syphilitic teeth.

This is what Frank had to tell us as the milk rose, swamp-
ed the table top and formed a cool clear lake of perfect
flatness, that sucked around the saucers and lifted them all
at once and all together until someone moved and sent a
ripple through the milk and the saucers floated away from
us one by one or circled on the spot according to unknown

currents, while small milk mermen with mouths like gup-
pies and fins like wings, grazed their way politely through
the wet sweet sea lettuce of our pubic hair.

★   ★

'You're giving me hallucinations,' I said to Stephen.

'Don't look at me,' he said. So I turned my face to the
wall and I slept like a baby.

Channel Surfing

I made the trip out to my parents' house and noticed that it was spring. They seem to have a monopoly on the weather. Everything was clean, with a little sharp shadow. The house was full of the ghosts of doilies, coasters and antimacassars that my mother threw out long ago. My father had been dressed in the kind of clothes that people go sailing in and you could tell that his underwear smelled of Comfort, or of Bounce. You might as well be clean, says my mother. I do not agree. Some people just have it, like a gift. Which is why my mother loves the spring, when people are seen for what they really are; when I look like something in the room is faintly rotting, when my mother looks freshly re-upholstered. It is because she has stopped growing I think, because it wasn't always this way. She was as bad as me when we were young. She was a slave to her washing machine and it didn't thank her for it.

My father was watching the TV like he was wired into the wrong channel. That is not the only mystery. The damage to his brain has freed up plenty. He looks around the room like it was the inside of his own head, like the electrics have escaped from the wall and are worming through the wallpaper.

'How are you Da?'

'Fine, fine.'

'Anything good on the telly?'

'There were some flowers on it, but they've gone.' My mother gives herself a little mental slap on the wrist and disappears out of the room. She comes in with a shallow bowl of snowdrops and puts them on top of the television set.

'How's that now?'

'Fine, fine.'

'Snowdrops.'

'Yes.'

'I just took them out for a drop of water.'

'Waterdrops.'

'Snowdrops.'

'Yes.'

'It's a mirage!' he said suddenly. 'It's a mirage!' He was delighted.

'Mirage,' said my mother, 'mirage mirage mirage mirage. No love, it's an oasis. They're in an oasis.'

'No,' he said. 'No!'

'I give up,' she said.

'What's a mirage?' I said.

'Over there,' he said, pointing to the screen.

'You can say that again,' I said.

'Over there,' he said, pointing to the screen.

'Don't tease him,' said my mother.

'How is he?' I said.

'I'm here,' said my father.

'Exactly,' said my mother. 'He, i.e. your father, is much improved thank you. And how's work?'

'Same as ever.'

'Nothing strange or startling?'

'Same as ever. Panic city.'

'Oh for God's sake talk to me.'

'Talk. Right.'

'I'm here all day with your father.'

'OK. OK. Just the usual. A few weeks ago one of our dates absconds, disappears and we miss the flight to Crete, so we had to send her to Killarney instead.'

'Could you not get a later flight?'

'We could get a later flight but we couldn't get a later crew. Film crew.'

'And the station full of them.'

'One each Ma. Maybe we could. I don't know. It was Saturday. There was no-one in except us. I don't know. Maybe.'

'Not at all.'

'Right. So it was Killarney. Except we'd already said on the show that we were going to Crete with a thing on sun-drenched beaches and the lot. So we had to cut all that out and I had to beg emergency dubbing and find Damien, haul him in, mucho pissed off . . .'

'Dubbing?' says my mother. 'Never mind.'

'You put it on horses,' said my father, 'like a bet.'

'Never mind,' said my mother. 'I didn't ask.'

'Right,' I said. 'So he came in to "Dubbing" . . .'

'You put it on saddles!' said my mother. 'You put it on saddles love. On leather.'

'That's not the kind of dubbing I mean.'

'Oh for heaven's sake! Do you think I don't know that? Living with your father it's like 2 down and 6 across. You could be patient, but you're not. Not even on the phone.'

'There's the phone,' said my father pointing to the television set.

'Shush now and let me talk to your daughter.'

The phone started to ring.

'Funny that,' said my mother, and went out to answer it.

I looked over at my father who was talking silently to himself. He stopped and glared at the television. There was a strain on the side of his face that still moved. I was suddenly terrified that he might be taking a shit. 'Ma!' I said 'Ma!' There was the sound of her laughter in the hall. I moved over to the television as fast as I could and started flicking buttons, to take his mind off it.

Some women in saris were smashing coconuts in a Seventies documentary, shot on film. 'In the final analysis,' said a voice-over, 'the coconut represents the Ego.' I flicked. 'Pull yourself together, Marlene,' said an Australian. 'The situation is not as grave as it looks,' said a politician. 'Pursuit of Love is thirteen to two at the off.' 'I told you so,' said a Plasticene snail. 'Yes!' said my father. 'YES! YES! YES!'

'What did you do to him?' said my mother coming in the door.

'I don't know. I think he might want to go to the toilet.'

'He doesn't say "yes" when he wants to go to the toilet. He says "canal".'

'What?'

'Well how do I know? It could be sewers it could be intestines it could be "can I?" it could be anal for all I know. He says it, and you don't know that he says it, because you're not here because you don't care. And when you do finally saunter in, all you can do is upset him.'

'I only changed the channel.'

'It could be "channel",' said my mother. 'And don't touch that television. It only gets him excited.'

She sat down. 'I'm glad you're here. You know I am. Go on with your story and don't mind me.'

'There's no story.'

'You had to go to dubbing.'

'Thirteen to two,' said my father, being helpful.

'Shush,' said my mother.

'Well we are in "dubbing", which is where the sound is mixed and you can add things in if you want to like extra applause.'

'Don't patronise your parents,' said my father. We looked at him.

'Go on,' says my mother.

'Go on what,' I said. 'Go on nothing. We just spent two

hours cutting out the word "Crete" and trying to stick "Killarney" in instead, but of course it wouldn't fit because "Killarney" is three syllables long and "Crete" is only one syllable long. So we tried saying it very very fast, then we tried saying it very, *very* fast, then we tried saying "Kerry" instead and it ended up sounding like "Kree" which is neither Crete nor Kerry and there was nothing we could do, so we all went home.'

'Well that was all right,' said my mother. 'I didn't even notice.'

'Well great. So where did you think they were going?'

'I just thought there was some place called Kree I hadn't heard of, I suppose. I didn't really think about it all to tell you the truth so don't annoy me now. It's all happened and past.'

'Well the airline is up in arms because I took out their free little ad, because we weren't flying them to Killarney, now were we? So now we're in breach of our contract and it looks like we'll be bringing them to Balbloodybriggan for the rest of the run.'

'Any chance of a holiday?'

'They don't sponsor personal holidays *mother.*'

'I meant any chance of you getting a break from all this, *Grainne.*'

'Yes. No. I don't know. They haven't told me yet.'

'Was that the show', said my mother, 'with that young girl in the orange tights and the custard.'

'You've got the colour turned up too high. Yes.'

'Did you not know she was pregnant? I mean could you not tell?'

'No.'

'I suppose you don't see enough of it,' she said, 'these days. A bit of a nerve really, coming on a dating show in that condition, don't you think?'

'Mother . . .'

'Anyway. So that was Stephen on the phone. He says he won't be there when you get back, he has to fly.'

'Stephen?'

'Sorry, did you want to talk to him?'

'How did he get this number?'

'Well you forgot it long ago.'

'Sorry. Of course.'

'Of course nothing. I gave it to him last week.'

'Shit, Ma! Double fuck and damn.'

My mother laughed.

'Regular chats now, is it?' I said.

'He does the horses for me.'

'What horses?' I said. 'You don't do horses.'

'Well today, for example, Pursuit of Love. A pound on the nose and first past the post.'

'Thirteen to two,' said my father helpfully.

'You know,' she said. 'I get a funny feeling about your father sometimes.'

'There's the phone!' said my father, and pointed at the television. *The Angelus* came on, with its picture of the Angel Gabriel and its electronic bell.

My mother dipped her head.

'Bong!' said the bell.

'Yes!' said my father.

'Bong!' said the bell.

'Yes! said my father.

'Bong!' said the bell.

'YES!' said my father. And the wig fairly jumped off his head.

Yellow Eyes

I come home from my parents and feel bilocated. My own house, not theirs. My own front door, that makes me wonder whether I am arriving or leaving somewhere behind; the key in the door, it's only me, the saddle of wood to step over. Mrs O'Dwyer's lino is still in the hall, though her ghost went into the skip, along with the armchair she died in with its stain of death, not on the seat, but on the back, where you least expect it.

The evening refuses to fade. The ache in the lengthening days is unbearable, making them feel dilated and unreal. My house was not made for so much light, it doesn't know what to do with it.

'It's only me,' I say again. There is no response. Stephen is not here. I miss him.

I have a spinster ritual that the house loves, so that going from room to room is like reciting the alphabet of my life. In the kitchen I start a pasta sauce and chop an onion and, like every time I chop an onion I think about the school-friend who showed me the right way to chop an onion, a remarkable thing for a young girl to know. I think about how she could never fix her luck, how people died on her, how disaster turned to good fortune and back the other way. Now everything she does is her own, while I stay lucky and out in the cold.

So I chop down from stalk to root and lay each half flat on the board, then cross-hatch each hemisphere as fine as you like, first down, then across. Each cut multiplies through the onion as I work back along the arc, like slicing time on a clock. And around noon, sometimes at eleven, sometimes at ten o'clock the half an onion falls apart. How many pieces of onion do you get? Hundreds — for sixteen slices of the knife — and luck does not come into it.

I put the olives in and try to remember the first time I tasted an olive. When the pasta is on to boil, I go to the bathroom and see my mother Hoovering the stairs. She pulls the Hoover up behind her, probes higher with the nozzle, then kneels on the next step. She moves like a caterpillar. She never kneels on a dirty step.

In the bathroom, I do my teeth. I tap the brush on the side of the sink and it is the sound of a man on the way to my bed. A good man, no less, though my body remembers him in its own way. So between the two taps on Mrs O'Dwyer's cracked enamel, with its stained overflow slot and its lost plug, I recall lying on the bed or sitting on the bed or standing at the window with my clothes on or off or in between (but always in bare feet) waiting for the door to open, waiting for him to see how I had arranged the first emotion and left the next up to him. Tap Tap.

I take my dinner into the front room and look at the wallpaper. Over the last month or so, the paper has started to come away from the wall. It is covered in big fat bubbles, like something surfacing in slow motion. When I first moved in I painted everything magnolia, because I said you can't make decisions just like that — a house has to grow on you. So it heard me, and did.

On the telly, Oprah is talking to women who gave birth to babies they didn't expect, who thought they had indigestion until a little bald head popped out.

'In a shopping mall?' said Oprah. 'Girl!'

'In a shopping mall,' said the woman. 'I was wearing a pair of shorts, and she just . . .'

'She didn't care,' said Oprah. 'That little baby didn't care what you had on!'

'That's right,' said the woman. 'She didn't even wait for me to get them off, came right down anyway and out one leg.'

The audience shrieked. Fat. I thought. Too fat for shorts. Too fat to know what was going on in there.

'I'll bet they stared,' said Oprah.

'I dunno what they did,' she said. 'I was too busy staring myself.'

In the corner of the room, on the outside wall, a seam of wallpaper has buckled and come adrift, seductively, like a button undone, or a scab waiting to be picked. I pull at

84

it in an experimental kind of way. Once you are started it's hard to stop. The paper is thicker than I imagined. Under the magnolia is Mrs O'Dwyer's wet dream of orange cartwheels — some designer dreaming of Tibet, ending up in Chiswick. Now I find that the cartwheels are only an excuse, because under that is what might have been a nostalgic chintz, but is in fact the very odour and idiom of murdered wives, of misery, the axe in the head and a corpse bricked into the wall.

Mrs O'Dwyer buried her husband long before she died herself with no-one left to claim her. 'A house needs children,' said my mother. She wanted to say that only a baby understands a carpet, that walls need to be written on, to keep them in their place. She wanted to say that there is no luck in it, but she is a modern woman and kept her mouth shut. Even so, her reproductive glee and Oprah's egging on follow me about the room so I strip the walls of the tatty, acid chintz and find the newspaper that was used for lining underneath. There are layers of the stuff, glued so hard and dry together you wonder what they were trying to keep out.

A sheet of the *Sporting Life* from 1939, yielded like puff pastry a scrap of newspaper advertising The Theatre Royal:

A Marvellous Spectacular Christmas stage presentation.

FEATURING:

MARCELLA SHORTALL, Well-Known Impersonator,

BOBBY MCDONAGH (age 10),
Ireland's leading Juvenile in Popular Songs,

THE SEVEN CASTILIANS in an Old Spanish Garden.

MR. CECIL O'SHAUGHNESSY, Eminent Baritone.

On the Screen
MARY ASTOR and RICHARD CORTEZ in
I AM A THIEF
(Premier Showing in the Irish Free State)
THRILLS! DRAMA! ROMANCE!

Over the mantelpiece was a bill from one of those butchers, where you take your meat from over the counter and pay at an antique cubby hole so that they won't get blood on the money. There is however, blood on the piece of paper, dried to a smeared brown, which means she got the chit from the butcher and didn't hand it in at the till. Or perhaps she paid all right and the blood came from somewhere else. She bought one lamb chop. On the back, in a female hand is a list: 'Chop. Chop. Chop. Chop. Cutlet.'

I move along the wall with an angry rhythm, feeling like I have been fooled and the paper comes with my hand in scraps or swathes. The plaster underneath is an old-fashioned pink and when I scrape it with the backs of my fingernails my teeth are set on edge, the follicles on my forearms contract in protest and the hairs stand to. Sharp edged flakes of pink stick to the paper in liquid shapes, blotting out words and phrases, or they fall off in scabs leaving the page pockmarked with meaning, or a piece shreds as I pull it off, leaving a central tongue stuck to the wall.

BROWN SCAPULAR OR AN"

"The Blessed Virgin, acco
   r blessed hands the scapula
   armelites a privilege, that
     R ETERNAL FIRE; that i
ICE CONFIRMED :
   is promise made by the Bles
   unbelievable. Yet it is true!
     ch confirm the reality of Sai
     t for several centuries, and fi
     o the present day.
CAPULAR INSTRUME
   an account of the Spanish W
   ers constantly poured in from
   capular openly on their breast
   assmate who was directly fire
   over fifteen minutes, an
   simply; "And here I am."
In this Spanish revolt against
   ular openly on their breasts. F
   victory was won, the first c
   "Go to the church of Our L
WHELMED WITH PRIV
   o-day, about *one hundred ple*
   capular Devotion, not to mentio
licable to the souls in Purgatory.

MEDAL FOR EVERY CATHOLIC

   e of angels, appeared to Saint Simon Stock,
   armelite Order and saying : This will be to yo
      R DIES IN THE SCAPULAR SHALL NOT
      dies wearing this Scapular will be saved."

     as "The Scapular Promise," is so wonder
     e historical documents, such as the one quo
     ion; secondly, the church has encour
     miracles and supernatural favours

Y MIRACLES :
   39) we read: "The Carmelite fathers of Sp
      describing the Scapular miracles. Whole re
      armelite Father showed the present writer a lette
      four machine guns, from a distance of 700 or
      token of gratitude to Our lady of the Scapular,
      940)
nism whole regiments of Franco's troops wore the
   dicated the fleet to Our Lady of the Scapular. Fi
   ssued to the triumphant troops marching into M
   apular and offer thanks for Spain's libera

   dulgences can be gained annually throu
   ntless days of partial indulgences, all of whi

esides this, a Scapular Weare   an, by the intercession of Our Lady hope to be deliv
urgatory on the first Saturday after death.This is the famous "Sabbatine Privelege."

Other things: A piece of a letter 'member your mother and I spent so many happy time   as a lark. We even talked about you! Yes, though that was to be many years in the future, nothing   e her eyes light up so much as hoping   t happen and that it would be for the best. There are many miles between us and I will never m   I know that the journey I am soon to make is not home to Ireland but to a happier abode (Deo Volente) when I can say to'

   4 persons. Wash well in salt and water. Remove the eyes an
  ith the brains and keep. If there are any clots of blood, rub
  overnight in cold water to cover. Place in a sauce pan.
  Uncover, skim, cover and simmer for 5 hours. Cov
  liquid into a basin. Remove the head to a board
  white sauce, mixed with brains, blanched, boil and
  minced.

FAGGOTS

1lb pig's fry including caul.   ha
8oz. breadcrumbs.   3
half teaspoon salt

For 5 or 6 persons. Soak caul in
saucepan with just enough w
the mixture bind. Cut caul
round to form balls
greased b
fagg
3

Stuck in the cracks around the doorframe are folded pieces of card. A couple have just one word on them; 'theopneust', 'dear', 'the Isle of Man'. On the back of a cornflakes packet, with the old-fashioned rooster just about to crow, a poem, by a lunatic. (I have to get out of this house.)

I met a soldier i   he Palatine
Who buffed hi   e till it did shine
God forgive him   hat he did.

He looked at me a lowly La
Said won't you stick i
Where all my gold is

I slipp
er into   ing
To pl   e him my only joy.

Instead of gold
As he had tol
I found a re   ment of toy
soldiers a g   nd piano an undertaker with a long face an
    operatic soprano with a loofah in her hand
and the rest of her in the bath and the corpse of Sergei
    Nijinski whose wake it was.

P.S. I know who The Woman Next Door is. Just in case you read this with your yellow eyes.

I wanted Stephen to burst through the door in a cleansing wind, his wings filling the room and a sword of flame in his hand. An oxyacetylene lamp might do. Either way, he was behind me now as I knew he would be, with a small laugh that felt warm on my neck and a copy of the *RTE Guide*.

'Read me my horoscope,' I said. 'And make a cup of tea. Or ride me. Or sweep all this shite off the floor. Don't just stand there.'

'Gemini,' he said. 'The Twins.'

'I'm not Gemini,' I said.

'Changes are afoot Gemini! That see-saw heart of yours knows what it is to hit bottom! Why not let someone you love sit at the other end and put you on top of the world again. You know who I mean . . . Jupiter is swinging through your third house and your luck is in. Clear out the old and sing in the new.'

So I tore the room apart, Stephen hovering at my shoulder in a state of celestial agitation. I yanked up the carpet with the newspaper underneath, stuffed it all out the window and when it lodged in the frame, went into the front garden and pulled, like a vet pulling out a dead calf. I fell into the flowerbed when it shot out in a lump and then wrestled it off me, the yellow scraps of paper blowing all over the road, landing in the neighbours' gardens, sticking to the hub-caps of their nice cars and sucking up against the holes in their wire fences. Let them read something for a change. I didn't care what they thought. They had been living with a madwoman for years and never told me.

I pushed and dragged the old sofa out through the hall, and tumbled it down the steps onto the front path. The springs made a tired noise as they gave up their dead; a collection of magazines chewed over by a mouse who had hollowed out a nest in the corner, when the good front room had been too good for anyone to sit in. Digested by the mouse, himself long dead, were: the face of a girl from a 1961 *Playboy* magazine leaving her smile, her industrial underwear and a G-Plan shelving unit; the hands of Saint Dymphna (I presume) patron saint of the insane; and the top of Gay Byrne's head from a picture that was thoughtfully clipped and saved.

I wet the floor and scraped the paper off with my fingernails, leaving streaks across the room. When the paste refused to yield I plugged a hose on to the kitchen tap and brought it into the living room. Stephen said Don't Do It, if only to urge me on and I stuck the end of the hose into his hand, went back into the kitchen and turned on the tap. I ran with the water along the hose and arrived through the door just in time to see it shoot out, hit the floor, bounce back off in a shower of correction marks and soak the television, which blew up, while two hundred and twenty volts arced back along the stream of water to Stephen, who also exploded. Two vacuums collapsing at once made the air feel suddenly thin. There was the smell of burnt wiring like a mixture of piss and sardines and the air held Stephen's shape for a moment, before expanding gently with the scent of ambergris and of toasted sesame seeds. On the floor, the hose leaked and bubbled.

No of course not.

And when I got up in the morning, the room was beautiful. Stephen had finished stripping the paper and had painted the walls white, working by the light of the moon and the light of the paint and by the glow that spreads across his face, whenever he gets a brush in his hand.

Breathing

'How was your weekend?' says Jo, when I come in the door.

'Stripped wallpaper,' I said.

'Sounds nearly as exciting as mine.'

The television in the corner is on with the sound turned down. There is a game-show playing through the static, a blizzard of lips and eyes. You can't even see the prizes.

'For God's sake,' says Marcus. 'Look out the window. What is that? It is a transmitter. What is this? It is an Italian game-show. How'ya?'

'Good morning. Good morning. Was that on all night?'

The LoveWagon mooches significantly by. She doesn't quite exist outside her office. Open space makes her look like anyone else, with a hangover and an itchy blue line on the back of one leg. I knew it meant trouble.

'Can I see you for a minute?' she said. So I went over to get a cup of canteen coffee — the taste of panic in your mouth, the taste of somebody else's panic heated over and saying 'hello'.

I go into her office and look at her nose, which is ordinary enough. It sits in the middle of her face like a nose should. The inside of her nostrils seem entirely respectable, though there is one mysteriously broken vein that trails over the small mound at the base of the divide. She is sniffing around, looking for someone to blame. It doesn't really matter for what. The audience figures are down, that will do for a start.

The LoveWagon's nose talks to her all day long and her mind has nothing to do with it. Her mind keeps her busy with other things, like how to win, like how to keep the monkey off your back. But sometimes her face goes very still, like a dog testing the air.

Winning isn't easy. She wants my sympathy for how hard it is to win. First of all she says the bastards are on our back again. The show is going to be pulled again. Damien has been making dirty cracks again, this time in Irish. Apparently there was a pun on Cumann na nGael and a windy orgasm, which none of us understood, so I didn't cut it out.

She played the joke as though I had never seen it before — stopped the tape, rolled it back, played it again — like a woman reversing repeatedly into a wall. This always made her laugh. Here was disaster on a loop, the gash we had made in time. The problem was more than political. I had scratched the record and made it jump. I had dug a hole we could not get past, nor stitch up.

She has a handsome face, but her hands are old. They look like string bags that are holding in the flesh by accident, that are accidentally the right shape for hands, a little map of wrinkles, fates and cicatrices. I could get sentimental about her hands. She talks with them because, being paranoid, she is afraid you might recognise her voice.

'We're up shit creek again. I am trying to save the show, here. I am trying, if possible, to save you.'

I wonder what her hands are saying. 'I need you — I need you all'? Or maybe she's playing with a knife, to see how real it is.

'From what?'

'I'm on your side, Grace.'

'I know that.'

Silence. I might as well feed her the lines. I say 'Things are shifting up there. Apparently Murphy is moving sideways and up and out of programmes altogether.'

'Which means we're finished. Murphy was one of the best friends we had. I know he shafted us at Christmas, but that was just a blind. He can't be seen to be on our side.'

'He's on nobody's side.'

'He is on the side of the ratings. Which is our side.'

'There's always McNulty.'

'McNulty's out. He's a liability. He only pretends to be on our side in case things swing our way.'

'I heard he was coming back in. I heard he's getting a push from Mahon.'

'Well if he is back in, then he's not on our side anymore.'

She laughs. She says, 'Grace. I'm afraid of where you want to push it.'

'How was I to know he said "orgasm" in Irish. I didn't even know you could.'

'There was that stupid looking vegetable.'

'Oh come on.'

'And it's not that either.'

'It never is.'

'There's a difference', she says, 'between showing a bit of leg and mooning at someone in the street.'

'Fuck them,' I said. 'They want it every way.'

'Listen,' she says, 'it will take Murphy just five minutes a year to grind you down. Some years he might forget. But five minutes a year to fuck your life up until it's too late and he doesn't have to care. He's paid not to care. Now as far as I know, he really does want this programme to succeed.'

'And I don't?'

This is a mistake. I should say nothing. There is more than one paranoid in the room and once you join in it is impossible to win. The television in the corner of the room has started to slide across channels. She is waving her sad hands in front of an aerial shot that refuses to cut, though sometimes it turns belly-up for a look at the sky.

'It is real Grace. You have no idea how much they need to be appeased.'

Five minutes later I am out of her office with no idea what real is, but knowing that I am to blame. My bladder is mysteriously full so I go to the toilet where I piss out more liquid than I ever drank in and I think that maybe she was just looking for sympathy after all. I think I should be grateful to her for some things, because I used to like the LoveWagon, I used to call her by her name. Perhaps she is no worse than any other. Perhaps television is just a crash-course in life and there is no such thing as blame. Then again, perhaps she's just a deceitful paranoid bitch who has it in for me.

The Most
Beautiful Woman

My father liked hairdressers. He liked to watch. I realised this when he took me for my first real haircut, not the kind of trip a father usually makes with his daughter, unless he is interested in revenge. I was ten and getting a sense of humour, which did not suit the joke on his head. I still hate hairdressers. I still fancy bald men. I should do a self-help book for women who get it the wrong way round.

It was a Saturday. The room was full of women in extreme situations. Their hair smelt like it was burning, their scalp was smeared with acid goo and they were flicking through magazines. They sat under the dryers with implacable faces. I wasn't surprised by the helmets humming around their heads, it was, after all, the space age. I was surprised by how ordinary they were, because you never saw housewives on Star Trek.

I wasn't distressed until Mrs Davitt came out of the backroom looking like a turkey, her eyebrows half-gone and her face shiny with insanity or a facial. Either way, she did an extraordinary thing. She walked over to my father and flirted with him. I remember her nostrils and how raw they looked — Mrs Davitt from up the road was flaring her nostrils.

My father took it like a bishop, his hands square, one on either knee, his face full of mischief. This is the kind of thing that upsets a child. My father was in the wrong place. He was no longer inside my head and once he slipped free the betrayal was comprehensive. (Man IN hairdressers IN wig IN madwoman EQUALS my father PLUS Mrs Davitt.) As if to prove the equation Mrs Davitt gave me a tenpence piece and a pat on the head before she made for the door.

I was put sitting in the chair on a pile of women's magazines, so I felt I might slide off at any second and land on the floor in a heap of horoscopes and Handy Hints with a pair of scissors stuck in my neck. The hairdresser's nails were long and red. Her hair was bright blonde and huge. Her eyeshadow was green and her lashes were amazing. She smelt of about six different things. I thought she was the most beautiful woman I had ever seen.

My hair was in her hands. She ran her fingers through it and felt the ends. There was something wrong with the ends. She picked it up again near the roots and pulled it down halfway, cupped my face at the chin, then shook her fingers free. One of her rings got caught and she gave the hair a yank, before she remembered herself and picked it loose, her fingers as careful and new as a small child's.

'Now,' she said.

She smiled at my father but I didn't mind that. They had

shared interests. Besides he was too busy watching her hands. Or maybe it was the mirror he was looking at, pretending not to check his face, or his hair, or the line between the two. When he saw me looking he gave me a wink. My father in the mirror was even stranger than my father in the room.

'It's her first real haircut,' he said.

'She'll be lovely, wait and you see,' said the hairdresser and I felt they expected something of me.

'So what are you going to be when you grow up?' she asked me. 'Would you like to be a hairdresser? Like me?' I didn't know how to speak to her. She had started to cut.

'I think that's a big secret,' said my father so that I could contradict him. My hair was falling on my shoulders and on the floor.

'I'm going to be a nun,' I said. The hairdresser laughed, which annoyed me because I was only trying to please. Nuns get their hair cut all the time.

'Or an astronaut,' said my Da. 'I wouldn't put it past her.' And I found him inside my head again. Comfortable and neat.

This is how the LoveWagon frightens me. I am frightened by the fact that I know too much and still don't understand. I am frightened by her nail polish, because her hands are so old. I am frightened by her room, littered with lost tapes and their lost lives — tapes full of real faces and sentimental cuts, like cut and rotting hair. Cut so it hurts.

What Goes Up

At home I play music because all the walls are white and because I miss Stephen who has disappeared into it. I turn up the music, loud and clean, let it scour me out. It fills the white room, then leaks into me, before overflowing through the rest of the house. An oboe segues up the stairs and slides back down the banisters, swells to fit the shape of the door and picks the lock, as though having a good time was the saddest thing of all. It wraps the chairs and flattens the mirror, mixes with the light and turns it solid. And just when I become this room made of music, always expanding, always the same size, just when I am inside and outside and cataleptic — I hear a breath, distinct and close.

There is someone in the room, or someone in the music, and I have the feeling that whoever they might be, they are certainly dead.

Another noise, this time from upstairs. Another breath close to my ear, *in* my ear. The oboe plays on, a little thinner, more withdrawn, the noise upstairs putting it in its place. Another breath, loud but apologetic — here I am — it is coming from the CD. It belongs to the oboe-player. If I played the track again, he would probably breathe again — just there. Which is little comfort as I turn off the stereo and listen to a silence more frightening.

From upstairs comes a muffled dragging, the sound of a man toting a sack full of body parts. Then nothing. I still hear breathing, but this time it is my own — or the sighing of the house, or the hot breath of the man upstairs, or the lungs of the corpse he has with him, collapsing gently.

On my way past the kitchen I hook my arm around the door and pick up a pot of blackberry jam, because a missile is safer than a knife. Halfway up the stairs I hear a wet rasping and sucking sound and the slap of something wet hitting a wall.

'Hello?' I say, because I am stupid that way.

Silence. The wet rasp-and-suck comes again. More silence. Whoever it is, he is in my bedroom. I lift each leg on to each new step as if they were prosthetic, cross the landing to my room and push open the door.

My bedroom wheels past; top corner left, ceiling, window sill, chair. My eyes are too wild to stop and look. In any case, there is no-one there. So why do I hear those slow footsteps walking towards me, across the empty room?

'Oh please.'

The footsteps halt. There is the same wet, rasping noise. For a moment I think it comes from my own throat.

'Stephen stop it. Is that you?'

A leg comes through the ceiling. I look at it. Another leg comes through the ceiling. The legs scissor once and the right one kicks. The kick brings a torso down, which hangs briefly at the armpits, before arms, shoulders, head, hands and a can of paint break through. They land on my bed, though the paint also hits the floor.

Stephen was painting the attic.

I look at the lake of white spilling off the edge of my bed and spreading across the floor. I look at my hand and find that I have dropped the pot of jam. I look at Stephen. He is sucking his thumb.

'I am bleeding,' he says.

'Good enough for you.'

'No. I mean *I am bleeding.*'

'Where?' There is nothing to show for it, one red spot sinking into the white of the paint, turning brown.

It is time to put my foot down. No more painting.

'What about the floor-boards?' I say. 'And under the floor boards?' Does he want me to take the tiles of the roof? What about the cavities between the bricks? Not to mention the plumbing, and inside the plumbing — I wouldn't put it past him.

A last bin load of Mrs O'Dwyer's scurf. A bill from Ostomy products in Parnell Street for something that I hope is out of date and don't want to understand. A poem about childbirth: 'The bigger the cock, the bigger the crown/ Because what goes up must come down.' All of this found in the hole over my bed, in between layers of wallpaper, vertiginously spread, with a gold and green pattern of repeating mermaids who, like Mrs O'Dwyer, had nowhere left to put a man.

Nearly the Same Thing

In the office, Frank shows me his wife, or he shows me pictures of his wife, which is nearly the same thing.

He says he never developed most of his photos, in case they turned out different to what he remembered, so they lay around the house like unposted letters until he rooted them out, brought them to the chemist and handed them over, with a smile as faded and hopeful as the chemicals, after all these years.

'And look at this!' he says, as if to show that, statistically speaking, he had always loved his wife, because most of them are of her — as if his eye always knew what his heart could not tell. They are not the usual conjugal snaps. She is not standing in front of the view with her hand on her hip and the sun in her eyes. Frank is good all right. His wife is often moving and the colours are blurred. He snaps her like someone you pass on the street. Very rarely, she has a sense of him there in the corner of her eye, but more often she is complete, private and uncomposed.

He tried to show them to her, but she shouted at him. At first he thought she was afraid of how she looked, or what she had lost. Then she slipped a cool word in. She said 'You didn't find the ones in the glove compartment, did you?' and Frank realised what it had cost her to leave the rolls of film as they were. She thought there was another woman in there, whom she did not know and did not want to see, a woman she could study for signs of her own mysterious lack. She thought that he had left them lying around as a temptation, as a dare — 'You can end it anytime. Just look in here.'

In the drawer on her side of the bed, in among the mechanics of sex, was a casing with the celluloid pulled right out, a curl of plastic, with thirty-six unconnected, connected moments that he had lost, whitening in the light.

Relative Density

Stephen develops a Band-aid fetish, excited by the possibilities of blood. I find him in the bathroom trying to shave, like a boy trying to grow stubble instead of down and he sticks little pieces of toilet paper on cuts that I cannot see. He is full of jokes. He has stacked the kitchen cupboards with Angel Delight. He feeds me rice dusted with saffron or with pollen from the lilies he puts everywhere, in old paint cans and milk bottles. The pollen is thick and smells of oriental sex, falling in the light.

He brings things into the house: a small girl who is in love with him, a horrible coy little thing who wants to help me tidy with her little toy dustpan and brush. 'Fuck off little girl,' I want to say. 'Go get a life.'

Up into the attic then to amuse this hungry little void, who simply pointed at the hole in my ceiling and said 'What's up there?' How do I know how to say no to a child? It is something you have to practise.

And it is quite a trip, quite a picnic, up among the raw

wood joists, the splinters and the dust. Light comes in from under the eaves and we lie down and look at the road from a funny angle. We look through the hole in the floor and see my bed, the duvet stiffened with paint. Fortunately she does not find the box containing a rubber Thing that looks like it might once have been inside Mrs O'Dwyer instead of outside. She does not find the glass eye that turns out to be a marble. She finds a doll. She finds Mrs O'Dwyer's doll. I check it for hexes and then let her have it. It is a nice doll, with a china face.

'Thank you,' she says. 'I think I will call her HANDBAG. After my friend.'

'That's a funny name for a friend,' I say with a dutiful lilt. 'Where does she come from?' 'It's a him,' she says. 'And he's a secret. And you can't see him even if you try.' As I said, Stephen is full of jokes.

He takes her into the kitchen and tells her stories about twins. He says that twins are good for wishes, like the fork of a tree is good for wishes, because the space between them does not really exist.

He tells her the story of two fat twins, who wished for the same thing only differently. The elder twin wished that she would always be slim no matter what she ate, and the younger wished that she would always be eight and a half stone. As the years went by the younger twin got fatter and fatter until finally she was so huge she couldn't see over her stomach to read the scales — which always, but always, told her that she was eight and a half stone. The elder thought this was great and stuffed her face to her heart's content until one day she fell through the floorboards and when they finally hauled her out, discovered that she was a very, very small two tons. The difference in their relative density forced the twins to hold on to each other at all times, in case the older should sink or the younger float away. They had always been close, but tensions began to surface in the relationship.

If they weren't different they were the same. Other wishes he could mention were: the case of the twins who wanted to be more similar, but couldn't really tell the difference; the twins who wanted one mother each; the twins who each wanted to be prettier than the other one, and who went from pretty to plain, from ugly to hideous, like a mirror in exponential decay.

When I come into the room, the child looks fantastically bored, so Stephen tells her that I work on the LoveQuiz. 'Oh.'

She loves the LoveQuiz, says the child, whose name is Aoife. She says it is fun, which it is. She says it is silly, which it is. She says it is exciting. She thinks Damien is really funny but he shouldn't wear leather trousers because they make him look cheap. She says she doesn't like boys now, but when she grows up she will like them and she will marry one — which sets me muttering.

'What is a lesbian?' she says.

'Ask your Mammy.'

I should take her into the office and show her off. Here she is. The national treasure. Here is the fragrant little scrap who skips through my rooms, making me queasy. She loves you all.

★   ★

Maybe I should bring my father in instead — sit him in the middle of the room, say 'Spot the difference.' Spot the difference between my father and my father. Between him and himself. Between his hair and his head.

This is a man who could only stand behind a camera — and even that made him uneasy. He took it out once a year and handled it like an animal, like it might turn round and look at him. There is something embarrassing about our endless black and white family Christmas, the children lurching older, one year at a time, the turkey staying the same. There is something embarrassing about my father's eye at the back of it all, the fact that we never stood in the sun. When you look at these pictures you might as well be him. You run your fingers through your hair.

My father hated cameras but he put a mirror in every room, because they forget you when you walk away. Oblong, square and oval, he knew them all. You could tell by the way he looked at them out of the side of his face, his eyes staring ahead like setting jelly. When I see one of The Brothers on the street I spot the look before I see the wig; the look that says 'I know that you are looking at it', even though you are not — at least not until now.

How could I look into the mirror as a child? How could I do all that milk-white budding breast stuff, eye-gazing, eye-diving and parting your hair six different ways? How could I fall in love with myself, when the place behind the mirror (the place where he lives now) was The Land Where Wig Is King?

But a girl has to grow up any way she can. There is a picture of us on our last Christmas, the one before the camera died. There is the turkey, mutilated and smug. There is the family smiling in front of the mantelpiece, making room for the tree. My father stands with his back to the light to take the picture. If the picture is to be believed, his eye is as wide as the window.

I am going to cut my knee, you cannot see this in the photograph. But first I will throw my plate against the wall, you cannot see that either. You cannot see the plate flying, the shove in the back from Phil, the grazed leg, the split hand, the simple way Brenda drops the camera on the floor. Look closely at our smiles. That picture is a black and white suicide. It is an accident waiting to happen.

It was me that got sent upstairs, of course. I was going there anyway. In the bathroom I sat on the edge of the bath, looked at my knee, looked at the floor and wept. The mirror stared at the door.

Everyone used to cry in the bathroom. You would think the acoustics were wrong, but none of us seemed to mind, there was something nice about being overheard behind a locked door. My mother would give it a casual tap on her way from one room to the next. 'Cheer up,' she'd say, 'we'll soon be dead.' Though she usually left Phil and his pride alone.

This time it was my father who knocked and the surprise

made me open the door. The sound of my mother leaked into the room. He was midway between two crying women.

'Take your time,' he said and smiled. His smile was for me, but his look was for the mirror where the wig was busy checking itself.

'Get out,' I said and looked at his head in a dangerous sort of way. When the door was shut I went over to smash the mirror. What was it that stopped me?

My jumper in the mirror was a pinker shade of pink, but the jumper in the mirror had no smell. In the mirror it all looked the same, except that it could not feel. Perhaps that was why the mirror was there, to witness the act without pain. Whether or not I felt pain was another matter. Perhaps I did not. Perhaps the pain was in the mirror.

I looked at my eyes in the mirror and I had the feeling, those eyes could see. I looked at the blood in the mirror and was afraid the glass itself might bleed. So I put some blood on the mirror, a smear of solid red. It separated us out. I thought, Now the blood is in the room.

★   ★

Marcus's brother came in to the office. He looks just like him. He opened the door and walked in, looking wrong, dressed wrong, with the wrong size hands and the wrong expression in his eyes. He looked like what he was doing was necessary and the right thing, but he still felt foolish and it showed on his face.

I knew that he was related to Marcus because they had the same delicate, wary eyes and I knew that someone had died because of the way he took his too large hands out of his pockets and then didn't know where to put them.

He knocked at the open door and just stood there while Damien pushed past him saying, 'Useless.' It is the afternoon of studio and Damien's exploding umbrella won't explode. Marcus is in editing. I am on the phone to Frank who was saying, 'Half an hour behind. Down one radio mike.'

'Boom it?'

'Thank you Grace. It can't be boomed,' and another voice says:

'Don't tell me. She wants it to sound like shite.'

Frank covers the mouthpiece and insults me for a while, which is what I am paid for. The brother comes over to a desk, sits down and stares at me, because he is surrounded by death and has to look somewhere. Damien is banging his umbrella against a radiator in an experimental kind of way.

'Come in under,' I say. 'Fuck them.'

'All arses covered so.'

'Every arse in the house.' The brother is still looking at me. I catch his eye like we're all in on the same joke. 'Except mine.' He picks a piece of paper off the desk, realises what he is doing and puts it back down.

'Useless,' says Damien, coming up to him, and he bangs the umbrella on the desk. The umbrella gives a small thump and smoke comes out of the tip. The brother laughs and then stops.

'Is that Damien?' says Frank. 'Tell him to get his fat arse over here, and stay on the studio floor.'

'You're wanted on the floor.'

'I'm trying to fix my umbrella,' said Damien.

'Your umbrella is wanted on the floor.'

I should say something, but instead I keep the phone in the crook of my shoulder and dial another number. Whoever is dead will stay that way. The line is engaged, so I turn to face him, a very busy woman. He asks for Marcus.

'It's his father,' he says, 'I drove down this morning.'

'Oh I am so sorry.' Busy but sympathetic. I ring editing and the phone is lifted. There is the howl of a tape rewinding and then close to the mouthpiece Marcus says, 'Yes.' And then to the editor, 'Just there. Back a bit.'

I offer the receiver to the brother, who gives an involuntary shake of the head. He is shocked. He didn't come all this way just to talk on the phone. I say, 'Marcus, could you come down to the office a minute.'

'Not really,' he says. 'Yes. There.'

'Your brother is here to see you.'

'*Shit*,' he says.

And I feel in the pause a reluctance, for which Marcus will always blame me. He says, 'And the out on that is "made my knees go kind of wobbly",' and then, 'I'll be right there.'

Pairings

That night I make a pass at Stephen, just for the sadness of it, and because he has started to smell like someone I might know. He has cut his finger nails and left the bits in the ashtray by the bed. I count them, because there is something about nail-parings that makes you check they are all there. And as I count, nine in all, I find that my problem is how to tell him that I love him.

I could tell him to put my body in a boat when I am dead and burn it on the water.

I touch his face in the dark and listen to his breathing tighten and lose its beat. I touch his chest and my hand seems changed by it. I float my palm along the air that clings to his thigh, afraid to touch, and the hairs on his skin rise to meet me.

Slowly, he lifts the duvet and slowly finds the floor with his foot. He swings around and sits up on the edge of the bed.

He bends down to the floor and comes back up looking

at the ends of his fingers. He has found the last nail-paring and now he drops it in the ashtray. I don't know now which disturb me more, the bits he cut off, or the bits still left on his fingers. His nails are thick, white and clean, the kind you see in films, when you know someone is going to do something unpleasant with his hands.

He looks down at the floor again, pushes himself away from the bed and walks in the dark to a chair in the corner of the room. He starts to talk.

He talks to me about his wife, about how little he understood. He says when he came home one day there were some playing cards in the snow of the yard and britches frozen so hard on the line, they near snapped in his hand.

He expected her to be gone, but she was there when he walked in through the door. He expected her to be gone and when he found her sitting there he knew that she was pregnant instead.

'It is a difficult thing for a man to understand,' he says.

The snow kept her warm. Like a drunk, the snow kept her white skin glowing even whiter as she grew, and the veins in her breasts and the veins in her belly spread like blue flames, licking her inside. She grew all winter, so white, and the hair between her legs grew in the spring, like corn. But it was the winter that frightened him, the white heat in the bed beside him, her belly drifting against the swell of her breasts like snow against a wall. Her blood sang in the bed beside him and the child, because it was a child, made her blood hot. The child was a stove in her belly keeping her warm and all he could do was put his hands there, before he shrivelled with the cold, as her blood hissed in and out of the child, that wasn't a child but a fire.

'That is what is frightening,' he says, 'not that the body dies, but that it grows.'

He came home one day, because he was always coming home, her body a sun he circled, always trying to see the other side. And he lifted her dress and put his hands on her because he thought his hands were not his own, they were so cold. The shock of his hands made the child jump.

The child kicked, he says, like a stone hitting a pond. He saw his own face in the whiteness of her belly then the child kicked and the whiteness of her body melted, like snow melts and he saw what was inside. He saw things lost, he saw things strewn in the ditches, he saw new grass and things that would rot in the rain.

But for a moment he saw his own face there, or some face. He thought that if he could paint he would paint on her belly, stroke by stroke and colour by colour, that face. He would paint a picture of what was inside, a rope in a ditch. He would paint a picture of his own face which was, just then, the face of an angel.

'It is a difficult thing,' he says, 'for a man to understand.'

How do you explain condoms to an angel? Or money, to a dead man? Or sex, to anyone?

'I don't think we would have a child,' I say. 'You being sort of conceptual, in your way.' He looks at me like I've lost my reason. He looks at me like he could make me pregnant just by looking at me. Like he could make me pregnant through my ear hole and no-one the wiser.

He tells me of the Angel Amezyarak who, with two hundred followers, copulated with the daughters of men. Children were conceived.

'And?'

'The angels are flogged every day in the third circle of Paradise.'

'So you do have circles in Paradise?' I ask, in the way that one might enquire about patio doors.

'It depends on who is looking,' said Stephen. Well silly me.

I ask about the children.

That night, Stephen sits on the chair by my door. If I could sing, I would sing to him. If I were a man I would rape him. I could cut my nails and burn them with his. I could cut my nails and plant them. I could walk across the room and touch him.

I lose my nerve and fall asleep, while all two hundred copulating angels slide down from the attic on to the foot of my bed and Amezyarak looks down through the hole in my ceiling and laughs, with his four wings and forty eyes.

Stephen has to run my bath in the morning, to get me out of the bed and the water seems sweeter than the sleep I just had.

'Bath. Sheba,' he says. He tells me that the Queen of Sheba was said to have a donkey's foot; that Solomon flooded the forecourt of the Temple so she would have to lift her skirts as she approached the throne; that when her foot touched the water it was made human again.

'Stephen,' I say. 'It is half past eight in the fucking morning.'

Now the Blood
is in the Room

Marcus comes back from the funeral. The country has made
him vicious and, for a few days, very quietly himself. My
heart goes out to him and this well of affection surprises
me and puts the whole office out of kilter — as if anything
at all could fall in to it. Marcus's silence is worrying. He is
only harmless when he starts to speak.

He is looking at me quietly when my phone starts to
ring. I lift the receiver and hear nothing but a distant
shouting from another line. Then a voice says 'Goodbye',
and it sounds like my father might, if he were ever let near
a phone.

'Is that you?' I say.

'No,' says the voice. It is my father and I feel like I have
been watching one movie and it has turned into three other
ones, all of them real.

'It is you.'

'Yes,' he says and his reasonable tone sends a dreadful

hope swimming like an eel down the line, the hope that my father has come back home.

'Alloa,' he says.

'Is the mother all right?'

'Motherwell nine,' he says.

'Are you all right?'

'Forfar, five. Fife four.'

'Yes,' I say. 'Is there anything wrong?'

'Hearts six. Montrose nil.'

'I know that,' I say.

'Cowdenbeath,' he says and hangs up.

'So am I, Da. So am I.'

The room is full of dead people. Frank is looking at his photographs. My father is whispering on the dead line. Marcus stands at the LoveWagon's door with his own father staring out of his face at me and smiling, with lips that say 'So what is life doing to me now?'

Damien stumbles in wearing a trench coat, a cigarette clamped in his teeth. What movie is he in today? *Columbo*? *The Big Sleep*? He looks out at us through his hangover and twitches, as if every move were a jump cut from *A Bout de Souffle*. Perhaps we have gone too far. I look to Frank but he is still with his photographs and seems to be stuck in a freeze frame. Jo has switched off. I just watch.

So this is the way the world ends, not with a bang but a:

'Goodnight John Boy,' says the LoveWagon, after half an hour of corn grits and whining.

'Goodnight Grandma,' says Marcus, who has finally made his move. He has spent the meeting making efficient little replies and conciliatory, useful suggestions. He has voiced carefully modulated concern about next year.

'We could do that next year,' he says. 'That's if . . . the shows goes ahead next year.'

He might as well have pointed out a bomb under the table. The eyes around the room invert, like the eyes of pregnant women, like the eyes of men who know they will survive, but not with honour.

He might as well have pointed out a bomb and said, 'Well I think it's just a suitcase.' No-one looks under the table. No-one looks at anyone else. Marcus looks at everybody, just for badness — because we all thought we were the only one to know about the bomb, if it is a bomb. We all thought we could get out on time. No point creating a jam at the door.

Except for Jo, of course, whose sources are excellent. 'Well count me out,' she says. 'I'm off to Sport.'

So it is real. The rumours are true. There will be no next year. It is real — some of us will go up and more will go out and they'll paint the set and call the show something else, like 'The New Improved LoveQuiz', or 'The LuvKwiz', or 'An Interesting Career Move By Someone You Have Never Met'.

'But hang on,' says Marcus. 'Is it really a bomb? It looks more like an opportunity to me!'

'Here we go,' says Frank as Marcus rolls up his sleeves, spits on his hands, takes up the hatchet and starts splitting hairs.

In the canteen the rumour takes hold. The show is axed.

We take our trays in silence and queue up for food that tastes like our own lives cooked up, cooled down and reheated. I have paranoid peas, with manipulated mashed potatoes and a web of intrigue on the side. Frank has Pork du Prince a la Machiavelle with chicanery chips and stuff-you-stuffing in a worried gravy. The researchers have Fuck You Foie Gras and Sole on the Dole. None of us can face desert.

We talk about Marcus. Everyone who used to like him doesn't like him anymore. Jo says,

'His father just died, for heaven's sake.'

'So?' I say.

I realise that I always disliked Marcus's father, dead and all as he is, which is another thing we could never talk about, because Marcus thought that his father was the most dignified human being who ever checked the sky for rain. He thought that he was still travelling towards him, expiating, vindicating, all that shite.

He used to tell stories about the old man, some humiliation at the hands of a grocer, some slight suffered in a bar, the conversation they had when it was all too late. He'd look at me and say:

'How can you get away from all that?'

Now he has nothing to get away from and nowhere left to go. There might have been something commendable about his journey — if you are interested in boy's journeys, which I am not. Marcus was always undergoing some kind of heartbreak with a woman he didn't love anyway. Every now and then, you'd hear him on the phone saying

'Sorry . . .' as if to say 'I just wish I wasn't so complicated', and the old man doddered out of his face in a disapproving, proud kind of way. Marcus's father hates us all and he hates me just for fun.

When we get back to the office he comes out of the LoveWagon's door in a post-coital haze. He is singing:

'Top Cat
The most effectual
Top Cat
Whose intellectual
Close friends get to
Call him TC'

But instead of baiting him, as I should, I find myself touching him on the arm. Shit.

The Mark

So I am beginning to feel the benefit of Stephen's care, his breath over my shoulder, the fact that he is clean. The white walls make the rooms look bigger and more deliberate. They have opened up the angles, made sense of the corners; they comfort me in the dark.

I look at his hair on the pillow, every shaft a miracle, every shaft still rooted to his head. Stephen dreams about his former life and his dreams are real. While he sleeps, he rolls through his death spasms one at a time. 'Like labour pains,' he says, 'but going the other way.' It is true that they are getting slower and further apart. Even so, it is hard to sleep as he reverses through a convulsion one pulse at a time, until his throat clears with a click.

As for my desire for him, it has left my crotch, eased through my body, surfaced to the skin and been exhaled, less a need than a breath, less a breath than a small bell, ringing in the silence. Maybe I am happy. Then I realise that whatever he is feeding me, it's two weeks since I have been to the toilet and I kind of miss it.

On Saturday morning he runs my bath, as usual, and the water, as usual, doesn't just slosh around; it whispers and ripples, sets pockets of light shimmering on the ceiling. A bird is singing on the clothesline, the water is singing in the pipes. There is no ring forming on the enamel. I can see the picture of myself, with lilies on the floor and on the windowsill, my shoulders rising out of the lion-footed antique where Mrs O'Dwyer had washed and looked at her body and found it good enough. Why not?

So I look at myself and everything seems changed under the broken angle of the water — paler, new. My front no longer breaks the surface to look at me like a quiet brown frog. My nipples have faded and there is something wrong with my stomach. For one thing, it doesn't seem appropriate to call it a stomach anymore. It is a smooth white belly with obscure functions and an iridescent perfect glow. Smug, that's one word for it.

The water plashes sweetly as I step out of the bath and make my way to the mirror, which is misted over in an opalescent grey. I wipe away the condensation, which is not a wetness but a fine web, a veil between me and the glass.

For a moment, I do nothing, because of the slight, rising shock. I pick up my nice ordinary toothbrush and brush my teeth in a humdrum kind of way. Hum goes my throat. Hum hum hum, and I have the usual conversation between the brush and my teeth and my eyes in the mirror, in which

I play all the parts. So I rinse and 'Tap Tap' goes the brush on the side of the sink and it is the sound of a man on his way to my bed, a good man, though my body remembers him in its own way, and I have my usual regret that he is gone and smile at the time I hit him because I thought he was the alarm-clock — violently, or so he said.

By which time I have no excuses left so I step back and lift my eyes to the mirror. O Jerusalem! The white breasts, uncomfortably high, the long, pubescent slope of the belly and my hands and wrists, my feet and ankles too slender to be much use anymore, with a sea-shell edge of pink where the bones protrude, a filigree of blue beneath the skin and a watery green and amber, an undersea shaft of light, hitting the iris of my eye.

I don't mind my body going, I said to myself, it's my sanity I miss. So I broke the mirror for a start, its silver shards turning to glass again. I needed all the bad luck I could get. When I called Stephen something in my tone of voice actually brought him for a change.

He opened the door and the steam rushed out at him in wisps, curled and wrapped itself around his head. He saw me and blushed a heavenly rose.

'Sorry,' he said.

'So you should be,' I shouted as he closed the door. When I pulled it open his back was turned to the room. I said 'I want my body back. I want my hands back and my cellulite and my stupid-looking feet.' It surprised me as I said it, but I missed the lines and the markings and the moles ticking away like timebombs. I missed my mother's knees and my Granny's hammer toes. I missed the subcutaneous ridges and drifts and all the mongrel contours mapping the history of this poor body and what it has been through — which is not yet enough.

A thought occurs to me and, while his back is still turned, I check between my legs and find that something ineffably floral has happened down there, something to which you could apply the word 'petal'. And when I straighten up again, my eyes more than ever sea-changed, Stephen has turned around and is watching me.

Which is when he touches me. I would call it a seduction, but who knows where a seduction starts and where it ends? Stephen raised his hand and brought it palm down in a benediction on my breast, which is the other word I was looking for.

It was like a seduction, in that the journey of his hand to my breast was unbearably slow, a mathematical uncertainty, that could never arrive, that is still arriving. It was like a seduction, in that the moment is still unravelling in my head. It may however, have been a simple hinging of the elbow, a failure of the joint. It may have been a memory in his hand that had nothing to do with his head, or his heart. It may have been a theological question. Why should we not touch? I looked at his eyes which were closed. I looked at his body which was surprisingly naked. Perhaps I groaned.

At least somebody groaned and it was the sound of everything giving way. I was just about to let slip the dogs in my gut, the bells and horns, the clamour and carnage, the Victoria Cross, the mourning, the ticker tape parade in my head, when I looked at Stephen's hand, now shyly tucked under my breast and I noticed that my nipple was gone.

I had never been wildly attached to the nipple. I always suspected it of some shocking subversion, the bizarre egress my mother happily called the 'expressing' of milk. If I wanted to express anything, I had always thought, I would do it in my own sweet way. But there is no doubt that I wanted it back, now it wasn't there.

'Grace,' he said and at the sound of his voice, which was rough and sad, I panicked. Which was lucky, because in my fright the slow motion of his hand bunched up and got stuck, a traffic jam in time.

So I had plenty of opportunity to consider the blind innocence of my left breast, its lopsided, sinister purity. I had plenty of 'time' to get annoyed at the unfairness of it all. Because although Stephen had no navel, being an angel and twice born, he still had two symmetrical nipples of his own, redundant, greedy, sharp enough to take your eye out, in a don't-mind-me shade of pink. Though who is to say what you might get out of an angel?

I look at them as time leaks on, cheerfully set in twin whorls of hair, the right travelling clockwise, the left the other way. Hair has started to creep all over his body and is more red than gold so that the light hitting his thigh looks like a personal sunset. It flows in a line to the blank spot where his navel should be and spirals there, each hair chasing and overlapping the next like water trying to go down a plug-hole, before spilling over and falling like a frayed rope to the geometric perfection of his crotch, where it seems to be holding something up.

So I realise that whatever is happening through the empty door frame, it is not all one way. The knowledge that the hair on Stephen's body is somehow my fault leaves me mute and glad. Because what could only be described as a hard-on of a celestial nature is craning nostalgically towards the blank space in the middle of his stomach, as though, without this marker on his body, it doesn't know where to stop.

'Sorry,' he says again. The sadness in his eyes is more human than I want to see and I know that however danger-ous this is for me, he has more to lose. I would speak to him and call him back, but the hand has a will of its own. As I stand there in dreadful one-eyed asymmetry and time drips on, his hand moves in gathering sweeps down my body to a place I value more highly — and I am resolved that no matter what he did to my breast, he isn't going to touch my belly button.

'Is this all right?' he says.

'No,' I say. 'No it's not all right.'

'Yes.'

'Stephen.'

'It's not all right?'

'Stephen.'

'It's all right,' he says. 'No, it is.'

And his hand inches on to a little piece of my body's infinity. 'What's a navel after all?' I say to myself, 'I mean what *is* it, after all. Between friends?' but I feel a pang, because my belly button is very neat. It disappears into my stomach and you cannot see the end of it. It has a certain playground kudos and the old-fashioned smell of a mid-wife's penny. I think of what it had been tied to — a dead piece of my mother and me they hadn't bothered to bury.

'It's mine,' I said.

'Please?' his eyes were beautiful.

'Fuck off,' I said.

'It's just a rope,' said Stephen. 'Just a piece of old rope.'

His eyes were back on the bridge again. I should have felt used, I suppose, but I just felt frightened for him. He was looking for death, but I did not want to give him mine.

'Remember Amezyarak!' I said. Which is just the thing you need to say when an angel drops the hand. It was lucky we were in the bathroom because his wings had caught fire.

Goodwill

Nothing can convince me to have a bath the next morning, nor am I able to wear a seat-belt on the way into work. I confuse left turns with right, indicate and go straight on. It is only by a miracle that I get there at all. Or, to be accurate, it is only by the absence of a miracle that I get there at all. I get there on the astonishing web of the ordinary that keeps the wheels on cars, the nails out of tyres and the sun swinging in the sky. I drive into work through the astonishing map of the ordinary, indicating fiercely all the way and when I get there Marcus is standing by the door, a little nub of flesh, soft and under used.

'You're looking well,' he says.

'Sorry?'

'No you are. You're really looking well,' he says, checking me up and down. I look at him more blankly than he knows.

'It's the skirt. Is that a new skirt?'

'No.'

'Suits you,' he says, failingly.

There is no way to get my balance. All day, things fall to the floor, slip out of my hands, the phone is a mess of wrong numbers. I say things like 'I think that's the breast option, don't you?' and people look at me.

The Monday meeting is real enough. Everyone looks at the LoveWagon's hands and keeps their own counsel. Everyone, that is, except Marcus, who stares out the window at the spring day as if he knows too much to be bothered. I sit and yearn, mutely, for my mother, among other things. The LoveWagon is talking about the importance of the last show, for us, for Ireland, for the future of broadcasting. She is ironic and paranoid at the same time. She makes jokes.

'How about it?' she says. I realise that she is talking to me. I realise that Marcus has turned from the window and behind him is a wide, clean spring day.

'Certainly,' I say.

Frank snorts.

'Well that's that,' says the LoveWagon.

I seem to have agreed, in my lopsided state, that the last show of the season can, indeed should, be transmitted live. Frank looks like his liver has fallen out on the floor. I have just agreed that nothing is impossible, that goodwill is stronger than death, that pigs would fly if only we could get them on the payroll. We are going out live, like the Mass goes out live, because you can't pre-record a miracle.

'It can't be done,' says Frank, but he is on his own.

'A few accommodations, a few changes,' I say. 'We'll pull out all the stops.' And the LoveWagon retires with a smile.

Marcus is confused. He looks like a man who is winning, whichever way he looks at it. He smiles at me because I have just sealed my own fate and he smiles at my skirt because he likes it without knowing why. I smile at him because my body is in a state of sweet, sick desire, though the rest of me is fit to kill. With the week underway he leaves me a note. He says he wants to have a drink. This is the worst of all possible signs. Notes imply an ending of sorts. Notes make me think of Marcus weighing up his life and deciding that it is about time he started sending notes.

I leave him a note. I ask to meet on Wednesday after he has finished viewing. He leaves me a note saying that he won't be finished on Wednesday until ten, how about Tuesday? I say that Tuesday is my studio preparation. What about Thursday? He says he is editing late on Thursday how about Saturday? I say I am on the ferry to Brittany on Saturday and even if I wasn't, Saturday was the weekend. What's wrong with Thursday?

'What's wrong with Tuesday?'

So by the time we meet it is too late, which is just the way I wanted it. I don't want to sit there and sympathise with Marcus for shafting me. I don't want to advise him that shafting me is his best possible, his only option. Besides, by Thursday I might have my nipple back.

No such luck. We go to a local pub. We could have met in town, but that might have looked suspicious. Marcus goes up to the bar and buys a drink. Blood money.

I sit and watch him at the bar. He puts one foot on the brass rail and catches the barman's eye. Then he catches his own eye in the mirror behind the glasses and the optics. What a good catch he is, with his casual shirt and his job in the media. He puts my drink on the table in a courteous way. If I brought him home to my mother, she might even cry.

The show is not going to be axed. It is going to be doubled.

'Game show one night, date show the next,' says Marcus.

'Same set?'

'New set. Two new sets.'

'There's posh. And after that, twice as much for their money.' When I get angry, my breast starts to itch. It feels like someone trying to get out from under a sheet a mile wide.

'One and a half,' he says.

'Like fuck. We'll be going live in half the time,' I say, 'because I'm a fucking eejit.' Marcus looks at me out of his green eye, then out of his brown.

'We have to stick together on this one,' he says.

'Why?'

I have a vision of Marcus in charge, trying to make it all *real*. I can see him in the kitchen at a party, backing a researcher into the counter, while he tells her how traumatic it is to go bald at twenty-four. I see him writing memos he never sends because he can't make up his mind if it is better to keep your head down or make a noise. I can see him putting it on the balance sheet of his life with a little gold star. I do not want to be around.

'What are you telling me for?' I say. 'I'm being hung out to dry.'

'You want it just as much as I do,' he said.

'What is there that I should want? It'll kill us.'

'Don't tell me you don't want it.'

'I have two days off a fortnight. I don't want it.'

'You want it all right.'

'You don't know what I want.' We could go on all night.

Because neither of us really believe and so we can't let go. There is no end to the fighting when you are trying to believe in something. All we know is that none of it makes sense, so you might as well win. Besides, it hurts.

'One show each.'

'No,' I say. And the night deteriorates as we both knew it would.

Nudes

I still can't wash at home because the water is not safe.

'It never bothered you before,' says Stephen, as I pour a bottle of mineral water into the sink and splash myself — a lick and a promise, that leaves a trail of bubbles dying on my arm. It bothers me now. Smells sit on my new skin like turds on a kitchen floor. Yet every time I clean myself, I become too clean; my arms more languorous, my knuckles more dimpled, my flesh so soft I am afraid it might tear.

So I take a towel into work and shower at the station, though I don't trust the water there either. I read the names on the dressing-room doors and pick someone who will not be in until the afternoon, a newsreader. I could become a very clean pervert, I could sneak people in for a fee — Shower With The Famous. Terry Wogan's bottom slapped against that wall. The stall is indefinably public, an empty archive full of all the flesh that was never shown on screen. It is discreet, blind, a television turned inside out. When you twist the knob you expect a voice to spill out instead of water.

'A crisis in the European Exchange Rate Mechanism,' says the showerhead. 'Minister of Agriculture moves on animal drug abuse', as I soap between the perfection of my toes and back to the soft handful of my heel.

'Bishop says no to Aids test.' There is no hair on my shin anymore. I soap the white swell of my thigh. It is not a modern body, wherever I got it from. And now it has no pubic hair.

'Ceasefire in Belfast,' says the water. I have no pubic hair.

I step out of the shower still itchy with soap. The dressing-room is a pornographic booth. The mirror is unembarrassed, wiped blind of all the faces, known and forgotten, who have talked into it as though half the country was watching on the other side; have stood there naked, looked into their own eyes and said 'Hello, and you're very welcome.'

The body that looks back at me is nine years old, or fourteen mixed with nine, or my own, mixed with all the bodies I used to have. I wonder if I am a virgin again. I should ask Marcus. He seems to know what it means.

It is while I am there, as the hammering starts on the door, with one of the nation's most trusted voices speaking to me in tones that would shock the nation, that I become resolved.

'What the fuck are you doing in my dressing-room?'

'Thinking,' I say. I think that I will stop washing and

dress in the dark. I think I will cover my body like the memory it is and just sweat it out. I think I will get my own back. When I come back from Brittany I will bring Stephen in for his audition.

The Audition

He got out of bed in silence; no singing, no Busby Berkeley routine with the toaster and a large sliced pan. He might have been nervous. He might have been suspicious or bored or transmundane. I would have checked, but my training got the better of me and I found myself treating him like a very stupid person.

'Don't worry, you'll be a big hit,' I said. 'Just give them that smile.' I was going to say 'Knock'em dead,' but stopped myself. I told him to wear the whiter of his two white shirts, buttoned up to the neck and no tie. Then I undid the top button. 'Perfect,' I said and told him to tuck his vest into his underpants and then his shirt into his trousers, so that he would be overlapped and interlocked from the waist down like a dovetail joint, because, I said, I have always found this a help when the going gets rough.

'Nervous?'

'I don't have nerves,' he said.

'Good.'

'I have doubts. I have the complication of perfect desire.'

'Well you should be all right so.'

I thought he might be fretting about going in front of a camera so I told him how Frank had said that he would jump bang through the lens and land in your lap.

'Exactly,' said Stephen. 'What happens if I jump bang through the lens and land in someone's lap?' And that was only the first thing on the list. What would happen if he stood in front of a camera and nothing came out at the other end? What would happen if *he* went through the camera and his electronic version was left standing on the studio floor? Or maybe the camera really did steal people's souls, in which case, would there be any of him left? Where would he go? There was also the problem of light. Would he be naturally overexposed? Could the camera pick up something as essentially ineffable as he, Stephen must be?

Which made me wonder why, when it comes to being on telly, everyone reacts in the same way.

'It's a bit late now,' I said. 'And anyway, you are supposed to know all these things.'

'There are so many places I could get lost,' said Stephen. 'There's at least three feet between me and the camera. And then what?'

'Then you hit the heart of the nation.'

'You know what I mean,' he said. So I told him.

'Three cameras. Right? You go down through the lenses, along the cables and up into the control room,' I said, 'where you get chopped up, joined together, whizzed along under a few corridors, round a few corners, into a room full of circuits that chew you up, split you up, run you through Presentation and bang you off the transmitter.'

'And?' said Stephen.

'You go flying through the air at the speed of light. Child's play. For you.'

'What kind of flying?' said Stephen.

'How should I know? It's a wave (it's a particle! it's a wave! it's a particle!). It's a wave, whatever that means. It's just a few little squiggly lines coming out of the transmitter.'

'No.'

'No. For real and in three dimensions it's more like a globe, with the transmitter in the middle. One globe expanding after the other, like an onion that never stops exploding.'

'Shit,' said Stephen.

'But you're still not on telly.' I was enjoying myself.

The journey to work was spent with Stephen dodging and feinting in the front seat as we picked our way through all the gory scraps of people and pictures that ricocheted off the road; waves hitting the ground at random, bouncing off traffic, sinking into pedestrians, getting eaten by cattle, drowning in Dublin Bay, or swinging past Jupiter on their way to the Horsehead Nebula. But some of them at least would end up wrapping the cablelink aerials and slithering down the wires into people's homes.

'There,' I said. 'Fame at last.'

'That's what I'm worried about,' said Stephen. 'There's nothing in those boxes, or a little bit of nothing. I could get lost in that vacuum. I could get stuck, in that little bit of nothing-at-all, in the middle of someone's TV.'

'Don't worry,' I said. 'You're fired across. They shoot you across, like out of a cannon.'

'Not me,' said Stephen.

'It happens all the time,' I said. 'It's not hard. It's not *you*. It's a signal.'

'You fool. You fool,' said Stephen. 'That's exactly what an angel is.'

When I reach the office, pulling him in like a sacrificial bull with eyes like plums and a garland around his neck, no-one takes any notice. I tell Jo I have an auditionee and she says 'Well what's he doing here? Ring up hospitality for . . .' and then she looks at him.

'Hello,' she says, mops herself up off the floor and leads him away.

I ask Marcus to take the auditions on his own. 'Personal interest.' Knowing that there's nothing he likes better than getting me out of the room.

The television in the outer office is on the blink, as if I needed to be reminded that Stephen is in the building. Jo comes back and fiddles through the static, trying to get a feed from the audition room. I do a running order, already a day late, while she shifts through a series of blank screens with a Bulgarian choir singing through each one. I think I see my bathroom in a music video with a river running over the floor. Some people applaud like Americans. There is a cow in a church burning her wet nose on the candles.

Jo laughs and twists the vertical hold. The screen dies. She starts to hum it back to life again.

'Oh,' she says. 'I know that place. I know that place. That's the place where I was born.' Which is when the LoveWagon comes charging out of her office.

'Who is that guy?' she says. 'Get him up here.'

Jo keeps adjusting the back of the set until the Love-Wagon realises that she works in an office and not in a soap opera.

'Jo, have you got the number of the audition room handy? I wouldn't mind having a word with Marcus.'

Attention does not suit Stephen. He comes back from his audition, passes me in the office, turns and winks by the LoveWagon's open door, which closes after him with a melting, metallic click and does not open again for forty-three and a half minutes. From behind it comes the sound of laughter, softened by the wood. The light shifts with a passing shower, the room shrinks, then dilates. Marcus smiles a tight little smile.

'Marry me, Grace,' he says, 'and I'll turn your money green.'

When the office door opens, they are both standing there as if they had never moved from the spot. The LoveWagon is smiling in a private way, as if we all like her and none of us are in the room.

'Just say the word,' she says.

'I will. Thanks Gillian.'

Gillian? When I have finished vomiting in the wastepaper basket I see the LoveWagon call Marcus in.

'What happened to work around here?' I say. 'What happened to the design meeting? I have to go filming and Staging is giving us horseshit about the trampoline. Graphics is out sick. Who wants to go to lunch?'

'In a minute,' says Frank. Stephen, unimpressed, is looking at the photographs which Frank is back to shuffling, like a gambler down on his luck.

'Anyway I've no fucking time for lunch.'

'Bring you back a sandwich,' says Frank, and the two of them walk out the door with a bad attempt at dialogue. 'So. What do you fancy for the Filly's Maiden at Navan?'

After a few minutes I follow them out, if only to stop that fucking stupid, sad fucking imitation that passes for fucking male conversation.

I find them in the canteen where Stephen is eating an apple. Frank is smoking, he is saying:

'Dungarvan, France, Disneyland, France again. Where's that? Jesus, Tubbercurry.'

'And these are the children?' says Stephen, with a curiosity that only I know to be biological.

'Friends' kids. Here,' says Frank, 'mother and child.'

Frank's wife is in bed with a new baby and a nightdress that looks oceanic. She is laughing at an older woman who is making an extreme face at the baby. She is wearing a plastic baby's dribbler, with a scoop-up base and a picture of Donald Duck. It looks hard and unpleasant against the tenderness of her breasts which have made the change from sexual to maternal, or tried to. The older woman, too, looks like she is in pain.

'And her own mother.' says Frank.

'Apron,' says Stephen, setting the picture on the table and taking up the rest. He shuffles through to Disneyland where Frank's wife is talking to Alice in Wonderland. She looks like she is discussing the price of sausages. Alice in Wonderland looks concerned about the price of sausages.

'Apron,' says Stephen, sets this picture on the first and shuffles again to a barbecue on a summer's day, this time with real sausages. Frank's wife is standing behind the grill. She has an empty green wine bottle in her hand, held up to her eye like a telescope. She is looking at the sun through the wine bottle and the top of the bib is distorted and green.

'Apron,' says Stephen. At which point I give in and go up for food.

When I come back, Stephen is arranging the pictures by lampshades. Frank has gone blank.

'Here, eat this,' I say to Stephen, shoving over a plate of chicken in puff pastry. 'It'll put hairs on your chest.'

'Lampshade,' he says. 'Lampshade. Lampshade. *Two* lampshades.'

'*Frank?*' I say.

'OK, OK,' says Frank, and gathers himself up and joins the queue.

'So how did it go?' I say to Stephen, whose palm is still open on the table, a stack of pictures weighing it down.

'What?'

'The audition.'

'Perfect.'

'No mid-air collisions?'

Stephen told me he had found out what it was all for. He told me that nothing hurt so much as being on screen, but that since it wasn't really him, it hurt something else.

'It was you,' I say.

'But I feel fine.'

He felt better than fine. You could see things in his eyes.

'Here she is in 1979', Frank's wife's torso is gently inclined. She is bent over in the way that wives in the Fifties hinged themselves at the waist in order to extract perfect cakes from their electric stoves. Her profile obscures the eyes and nose of a crying child. The child is in motion. Its two hands are helplessly extended and flinging dirt through the air.

'You have to strip them down,' says Stephen.

'She's leaving me,' says Frank to no-one.

'You have to peel them away,' says Stephen, 'one layer at a time.'

'Leave him alone,' I say.

'Don't worry about me,' says Frank. A wet skin of tears has formed on his eyes. How can I help him when my own body is a blur? How can I help him when Stephen is leaving me?

'Hang on,' says Stephen. 'Try turning them upside-down.' He sets the photos on their head and gazes at them as if they finally made sense. And it is true that somewhere in this tangle of colour is a thin film of awareness. She wants him, whether or not she knows he is there.

'At what?' says Frank. 'The lampshade?'

When I get back, the LoveWagon is sidling around the office, bumping her hip off the side of desks and reading whatever is lying there with a careless, downward glance. Marcus is standing with the phone wedged between neck and shoulder and a sheaf of papers in his hands. It is the way he shoots someone if he wants to say that they are 'highly' successful. Sometimes I think that there is no-one on the line.

'Is he yours?' she says, in her girlie voice.

'No,' I say.

'Lucky you.'

After the Audition

Stephen is exhausted. He has a fever and I put him to bed. The heat coming off him is physical. The sheet stays a few millimetres off his skin and will not be smoothed down. I blame the canteen food and he does not bother to disagree. His sweat smells. He asks me to take the lilies out of the room.

He asks me to take the mirror out of the room. He asks me have I ever looked closely at a wall after you take a mirror down — how blind it looks and how knowing.

My poor sick angel. It makes a change, to look after him instead of the other way round. I hold his hand, because that is what you do when someone is sick. Or is it? All I can see is the radiant madness of his skin as he sweats into the dusk. It seems that I do not have a gift for illness. I practised on animals when I was small, and they all died.

My father hated pets so we saved up for hamsters and brought them home as if by accident; hamsters, mice, anything small or furry or happy. Though they never really looked happy in our house, it has to be said. It was not all my fault. Phil was quite cold towards them and full of scientific curiosity. When the first cat died, leaving us a bagful of kittens, Phil said she died of a hole. I thought he put it there himself.

There was also a broken-winged sparrow who shat all over our hands. We didn't mind that either and put it in a cardboard box.

'No,' we said, 'don't you touch him', as we picked him up, 'he's sick.' Then the sparrow died.

Some of the hamsters started going insane, just like people might. We put sherry in their drinking water to calm them down, but they just kept on mounting and biting their brothers and sisters, their daughters, nephews, grannies, cousins, their own front legs — and the drink had nothing to do with it. I didn't know that sex had anything to do with it either. I dropped the small ones down my shirt for fun. They ran around in there like my breasts might, or like the hands that would feel them. I didn't know they were mad. A few more corpses every morning and then the whole lot disappeared. We were used to it, in a way.

Then my mother went into hospital, just like having a baby. Who looked after us? I cannot remember. It must have been my father, tying shoelaces, combing hair, buying things with instructions on the packet. He might have bought us lemonade. Surely I should remember fish fingers and lemonade and wearing the same clothes all week? Surely I should remember him dumping us in the bath, three at a time and drying us with the wrong towel, how many children at a time, rasping us with the biggest roughest towel until we shrieked.

It was not a baby. It was benign.

My mother did not believe in frightening girls, she thought it would give them menstrual cramps when their own time came. Still, we knew about the wrong thing in her tummy. It must have been the neighbours whispering over cups of tea with the door shut. The size of a ping pong ball. The size of an apple. The size of a fist. There was a whole shop in there, the size of a piece of fruit. There was a whole cathedral in there, the size of your head. Wide shot, close up, wide shot, close.

What I remember is not so much the size but the hair. That is what they whispered. It sweated as it grew and put out hairs. Those are the easy ones to catch. You know they are harmless if they grow hair and maybe a tooth (maybe a smile). Of course it made sense.

I knew where she got it. I knew what had put the hairy thing in her tummy. It was not my father at all, but the thing on his head. This was why it hurt her. Why it was not a baby. We were right to be afraid.

Stephen says 'Tell me something good for a change. I am tired of all this.'

'Like what?'

'Something to rest my mind on.'

'Give me my body back. You can rest on that.'

'I am tired of all this,' he says. 'I didn't exactly ask for this.'

It seems that I am set to lose him, one way or the other. I am filled with the shame that happens with strangers, as if I had shown him something, but he had not noticed. As if I had shown him something and he did not care. What sort of an angel was he anyhow?

'Am I so bad?' I say.

'Am I so bad?' he says.

'Stop that,' I say.

'Stop that', and he turns his back to me, hefting the sheet over with him and bringing it too far, so that a line of piqued flesh lies exposed, sunk into the mattress.

I sit there as the sun sets. It moves through a tear in the cloud and shadows lash out from the roots of the furniture, making things look old and tenacious. Stephen's hair flares gold in the light and sets a faint hum of colour around his shadow on the pillow. I do not mind him having a halo. I just hate the way it comes and goes.

Tell me something good, he says. And because I am helpless I tell him of the day I learnt about clouds, sitting with my father on a hill in the woods where you could see out and not be seen, watching the light and dark chase each other across the countryside. My father looked at the sky and I looked up with him and saw how high the clouds were off the ground and how much higher the sun. I looked at the ground and back at the clouds and realised all at once about angles and light, about wind and distance. I realised that things did not have to touch the ground in order to throw a shadow.

I pointed at the dark patches running across the ground, said 'Look, it's the clouds', and laughed. I remember my father looking back at me in the sad, amazed way parents have when they realise the distance between the world and their child.

'Did you never see that before?' he said. As though my seeing it made all the difference.

'Hunph,' says Stephen.

'Not good enough?'

'Fine,' he says.

Stephen's wings shift under the sheet like stumps. I am so distressed I cannot speak or move away. I sit by the bed as the dusk closes in, then clears again into night. And when the moon comes to the window, I watch the reflection of the glass on the wall, until it goes.

Seeing Yourself

I know her as soon as I walk into the room, this girl who might claim my angel, this girl who might, on a whim, turn into me. She is sitting quietly and smiling. Her eyes are bright and her legs are crossed. She looks like someone I know, but that doesn't worry me. We choose them for it. We say 'I have a Julia Roberts type, except for the mouth'. She looks like the girl-next-door because she is supposed to look like the girl-next-door. She looks like everyone else we've ever had on the show, but this time, it doesn't calm me down.

They go through their camera tests while I work on a new game for the biggest, the best, the last show of all, looking up now and then so they will think I am paying attention. People do not watch the television, they fight, feed the baby, read the paper, until something catches their eye.

She catches my eye all right. Warm voice — lower middle — receptionist — basketball — nightclubbing — anecdote —

left job to travel — funny anecdote — wants to work with relief agency. Damien: 'What kind of *relief* are you talking about?' Doesn't walk out. Laughs 'naughty boy' laugh with a bit of 'would you ever cop on to yourself' on the side. Perfect. Eyes a bit too glittery.

I go over to her and introduce myself. She thinks that she hasn't got the gig because Damien is on the other side of the room. I tell her that I am in charge. She smiles and adjusts, taking comfort in the state of my clothes.

'A bit nerve wracking,' I say and she glances down at her legs, at the line where they are bisected by her skirt. There is something a little too orange about her tights, or too orange, perhaps, about her legs. A dodgy fake tan slapped on in a panic, because the camera never lies.

'You could say,' she says.

'You did well.'

'Great.'

'Now tell me, what do you like about the show?'

So she did, and it all seemed very reasonable, if this weren't the woman who was going to steal my angel away from me. So I ask the question that we never ask, though we do give them all a little speech about good fun and goodwill. I say 'You don't have a boyfriend, do you?' and she says 'No' in a way that tells me she is lying, though it takes more than one lie to describe most of the relationships I know. Whatever the story, one lie is enough for me.

'Well Edel,' I say, 'you've got the gig', and she is thrilled.

I stay to fix a wardrobe call. 'Bring in some clothes and we'll have a look.'

'You want me to wear my own clothes?' she says and there is more than the usual panic in her voice, more than the usual coy 'Oh I couldn't possibly', that you leave outside the door if you want to be on TV.

She looks up at me and I do not know what she sees. Nothing is my own anymore. She might see herself. She might see the pity I feel, for no reason at all. It is when I remember my own body, sad, sweet and blank, that I know what I wanted to say to her.

'Have you . . .? You haven't been on the show before?'

'Sorry?' she says.

'I'm sure I've seen you on the show before.'

'In the audience?'

'No.' It was a bare moment.

'On the show?' she says.

'Yes.'

'Not me.'

'Oh good. You're not called Marie Keogh, are you?' I was not being polite. But although I had gone too far I never expected her to say:

'Is that her name?'

So I wasn't the only one. She herself was sitting watching the telly one night when she saw someone who looked just like her in the audience of The Late Late Show.

'It must be somebody else so.'

But that was only the start of it. She also saw herself answering a question about European union in a vox pop in Henry Street.

'Maybe it's someone who looks just like you.'

'Yes.'

'Or what . . .?'

'She is wearing my clothes.'

'She is wearing your clothes,' I say.

'But different.'

'Different.'

'Different combinations.'

'Right.'

'It's not me,' she says. 'Really. Ask my boyfriend. He saw me on Questions and Answers when I was away in Spain for two weeks. Talking about the Beef Tribunal. What do I know about the Beef Tribunal? I didn't even have a tan.'

'I thought you didn't have a boyfriend?'

'Well not any more,' she says. 'Obviously.'

Then she saw herself on the LoveQuiz. What really annoyed her was that this woman dressed better, even though they wore the same clothes. She accessorised.

'I keep buying scarves,' she says. 'But I can never wear them right.'

So she cut her hair short and dyed it blonde and sat down to write to us personally. And here she was. She produces a driver's licence. 'Edel Lamb' it says.

'Fair enough,' I say, because you cannot fold a flood, and put it in a drawer. Besides she doesn't look pregnant — and my mother is always right about these things.

Getting Notions

'Grow, grow, grow, your goat, gently down in Sneem.' My father is singing when I come home. I never knew he could sing.

'Of course he can sing,' says my mother.

'Well there's a turnip for the books,' I say and she says, 'Grainne, one of you is bad enough.'

'When did he stop singing?'

'What do you mean stop?'

'Well I never heard him before.'

'It's not my fault,' she says, 'you forget all the good things.' And from the front room comes a plangent baritone that I can't even imagine coming out of my father's face.

'He sounds in great form.'

'Yes,' she says, a little warily ('Warily, warily, warily, warily, siphon off the cream').

'So what's the latest?'

'Oh nothing new here.'

'Well he's singing at least.'

'Yes.'

'Anything strange or startling?'

'No. Grainne. Nothing strange', and she laughs, as well she might.

'Any improvement?'

'Well, he reminds me more of himself. I suppose.'

'That's good.' And this sudden breach of the privacy that surrounds marriages and sickbeds makes me familiar.

'In what way. What way do you mean?'

I look in to the sitting room to say hello. My father is sitting in the wing-chair in the space between the door and the window. He is wearing a coat and hat, with one of my mother's silk scarves around his neck and another around his wrist.

'There's something different about him.'

'Would you say?' says my mother, making me feel like I am six years old again, trying to fix the difference between her words and the smile on her face.

When my brother Phil arrives we all sit in the sitting room and talk over the sound of the television, the way we did as children, except that when we were children my father did not sit in the corner and croon, I don't care what anyone says.

We grew up a few years ago and started to look at each other when we spoke, which was always somehow surprising. It was Phil who started it. After he got a job and a flat Phil would walk across the carpet and turn the television off — a self important gesture, we thought. Tonight however, Phil seems as keen as anyone to sit and hoot at the ads, shout at the news and tell me the graphics are wrong again. All of which I find reassuring. It means that I am not the only one who has noticed.

Because if it comes to a choice between watching the television and watching my father's wig, the television wins hands down. The choice is made easier for us by the fact that the wig has grown since the last time we saw it and we don't want to mention this fact to each other, no matter how loud or entertaining the programme might be. We don't want to look at my father's wig long enough to see if it is still growing; say a half an hour, plus commercial break. We don't want to find out whether the wig has just started to grow, or just stopped growing. Which is to say, we want to find this out urgently and with every straining optic nerve; with every orbital muscle and cord of tissue that keep the eyeballs, as we have discovered, so tenuously in our heads.

We watch the news and I tell my mother that the reporter once threw a typewriter out of a first-floor window at her lover who was leaving the building. Then we watch the ads and my mother says 'How much would he get for that now?' and I say 'I dunno. Loads.'

Then we watch a chat show and Phil says he saw the host going into Brown Thomas's last Christmas which is my cue to talk about his sex life and my mother's to say 'I don't think he would sleep around, he's far too clean', and mine to say 'Maybe he does it in the shower.'

These are old conversations, but it is difficult to be

original when there's a wig growing in the corner of the room and the man under it is laughing his head off.

'Why do you not do any *good* programmes?' says Phil as the chat show switches from amputees to disco dancing champions. 'Hot on the heels', says the presenter, 'of their recent success.'

'WAVE!' shouts my father. 'Do you remember Josie?'

'This is an excellent programme,' I say.

'It's awful,' says Phil.

'Married that guy in Jordan before he left her,' says my father.

'Awful,' says Phil. 'Look at that woman's backside. Who was responsible for that? Who was responsible for letting that backside on, in pink lycra?'

'You want beautiful?' I said. 'Look in the mirror. You want good telly? It's the woman down the road making a show of herself.'

'Poor Josie,' says my father. 'Cad a dheanfaimid feasta gan Ahmed?' My mother starts to laugh. She says 'Yes I remember Josie.'

'Well there you have it,' says my father and she laughs again.

Phil and I start to panic. We turn up the volume.

'Tatty,' says Phil. 'Condescending. Self important.'

'You want self important? Look at you. In your Armani knickers because you can't afford the suit.'

'Under where?' says my father.

'Here it is,' says my mother, for no apparent reason and puts her hand on his arm.

160

'People don't want the telly getting notions,' I say. 'They just want some company out of it, a bit of gossip, a bit of drama, a sing-song around the piano.' In the corner of my eye, I see my father's wig creeping imperceptibly down his neck.

'You don't even believe that. Look at that nonsense,' says Phil, who sees where my eyes have strayed and wants to fix them back on the set.

'So? It's my job to believe it,' I say.

'You wish.'

Upstairs my mother finds me looking at a new picture on the wall. It is a picture of her, with a baby in her arms. The baby is me. She sits in the grass and holds me up for the camera, mother-love in her face and love for the person taking the picture in her eyes.

'Why did you put that up?' I say to her.

'Grow up, Grainne,' she says, on her way to the bathroom.

'I'm in that picture.'

'I would have thought', she says, 'that was the point.'

'Who took it?' I say. 'Did Da take that?'

'Who do you think?' she says as she closes the door.

She stays in the bathroom too long, while my father sings downstairs and Phil sits in silence. My mother cries privately but with no shame. She cries easily, because it is her right to cry, in her own bathroom, in her own life. She cries quietly, and with abandon, because her tears, like her children, are her own.

Downstairs the chat show has shifted to a half hour about the Shannon. Local people stand up in the audience to be on the television and to be counted.

'Hydroelectric Scheme,' says the television. My father starts to croon.

'Airport,' says the television. He breaks into song.

'Satellite link,' says the television, a dream my father had, hanging in space while the earth rolled under it.

'The pale moon was rising,' sings my father. 'Above the cream fountain.'

And suddenly there is a choir of girls singing with him in three-part harmony: the serious altos in their velvet dresses, the gamey mezzos with their air-hostess eyes and the poor, glorious soprano, her lips grasping the high notes like a horse picking up a polo mint. They sing to break your heart, the Flower of Irish Womanhood, their eyes true, their hands sweaty, their virginity as real as Irish Coffee. (Why not?)

In the corner of my eye I see that I was mistaken. The wig has stopped growing. The wig is not growing anymore. With a bit more effort we might realise that it was always that length, ever since we were children. Then the wig starts growing again.

And all the time, stretching and twisting between myself and Phil on the sofa, is our childhood, in three-ply.

Revenge

The beginning of revenge is the childhood body, its milk white parting. Marcus and I sit at either end of the office, with one childhood each. It seems a fair distribution.

I nearly like my new girl's body, whose sweat doesn't smell anymore. I might as well use it. I take it with me into the LoveWagon's office and sit it in a chair. I put my hands under my thighs to keep myself from fidgeting and I resist the urge to blow bubbles with my spittle, pull my skirt over my face or ask her for money. She is banging her remote control on the desk. If she turns it on me I might just disappear.

The television breaks into life. She has been watching the audition tape. Stephen looks out of the screen at us, frozen. A frame bar scrolls upwards across his face, rewriting him each time.

'So what are you saying?' says the LoveWagon. It is a good question. What I am saying is as big as the room.

What I am saying is all around me so I can only say it one piece at a time.

'It's not fair!' That is what I am saying. She looks at me.

'Fair,' she says softly, nostalgic for the thing itself. 'Fair' as if it were a word she hadn't heard in years like cack, or poo, though the people around her were always talking shite.

'I'm saying that I can toe the line. All right?' What did I say?

'Nothing lasts for ever, Grace.'

'Nothing lasts for ever, and when it comes to the crunch I can toe the line.'

'By the time you see the crunch, it has usually come and gone.'

Her hands are very mannered, very careful. She is presenting the news for the deaf in slow motion. Behind them, Stephen has, not inappropriately, started to laugh. 'Huh' he says.

'You could have told me.'

'I told you they were serious. I was blue in the face telling you.'

'But not so I knew what you were talking about.'

'Aw,' says Stephen, stopping and lapsing again. 'Aw. Aww. Awww. Hhwawh.'

'I named this show,' I say. 'I made the difference. Tell me something on the show that I didn't do, that Marcus did.'

'No-one doubts you.'

'Awh. Uh Hwuh.' It is crawling out of his face like an exorcism.

'What are you talking about?' she says. 'What do you want?'

How can I say what I want? I just don't want to be left behind, while Marcus goes out to buy six new shirts or she floats upstairs like Mary Poppins on her non-stick backside.

'Hujhhawarrrr,' says Stephen.

'It's only a rumour anyway,' she says.

'You told Marcus it was all decided.'

'They have decided it may happen.'

'Wuh. Huh,' says Stephen on the screen.

'It depends on us. It depends on you.'

'Hwuawrghh. Huh.'

'What do *you* want? You can get anything you like around here. If you don't let the uncertainty get you down. Seriously. Work with the confusion. Not against it.'

'Anything', said her hands, 'you want.'

She does not know what I want. She does not know the meaning of the word 'confusion'. With all her this-or-that, her either-or-and-both. When I was a child I wanted other girls' bald-and-hairy fathers for my own. But I didn't get them either.

'I want the Dating Show.'

'And? Any ideas?'

Why should I give her my ideas? She knows better how to use them than to have them. Still, I lean over to the VCR and make it work with the touch of a few buttons, like a child.

'Here's my presenter, for a start.'

'Oh,' says the LoveWagon while Stephen, released, slips into his laugh of celestial gaiety.

I leave her looking at the tape. Stopping it, rewinding, playing the laugh again. Stop. Rewind. Laugh. Stop. Rewind. Laugh. Stop.

At the door I remind her that Marcus might know about humiliation but he can't handle sex.

'He's very good at the games,' I say and we both smile, though who is to say what she finds funny? I go to the toilet and piss her out. I piss out Stephen's stop and start. I piss myself, with my new child's bladder, urgently, easily, back into the flow of time.

Half

When I get back, Stephen is nicely insane. How can I tell you half the things he said?

'Good evening Ladies and Gentlemen,' he said that a few times.

'Good *evening* Ladies and Gentlemen.'

'*Good* evening Ladies and Gentlemen.'

'Dia dhiobh a dhoine uaisile agus failte roimh.'

The whole house smells of depilatory cream, the maddest smell I know. Stephen has acquired himself a tan and some more teeth.

The washing machine has been going for a week and the place is full of sheets. Stephen cannot fold them on his own. I pick one up and am amazed. He has never folded a sheet with someone else. He has never stood at one end of the room, with two corners of a sheet in his outstretched arms, never brought the ends together, held one arm high and dropped the other to pick up the fold. He has never walked the length of the sheet and handed over to the person at the other end, stooped to pick up the new fold, walked half the length again, handed over again.

We get tangled. He hands over the wrong face of the sheet to me, the left corner in his right hand and the right in his left. He doesn't care that when he stoops, there is only a knot, swinging by the floor.

There is nothing I can do. I am two years old again. I want to lie down on the clean sheets and show him my stomach. When he walks across the room I want to take his hands, walk up his legs and do a somersault.

He takes me upstairs and shows me what he has written. He has made a list of errors.

Errors:

No. 1) That Isaac couldn't tell his kid from a goat.
No. 2) That the Isle of Man is bigger when you are on it.

My mother rings. She asks to talk to me and I take my thumb out of my mouth.

'Hullo?' I say into the receiver as though there might be a big mystery in there.

'So how's Grace?' she says.

'Hullo?'

'Yes,' she says, a little testily. 'Are you all right?'

'No,' I say.

'Are you all right?'

'No.'

'I can't leave your father,' she says. 'Put me on to Stephen', as if he hadn't started all of this in the first place.

'*No.*'

'Can you get some sleep?' she says. 'Are you sleeping?'

'Sort of.'

'Try and get some sleep.'

'OK.'

'Will you?'

'OK.'

'Will you?'

'I said OK.'

'How's work?' she says and then changes her mind. 'Try and get a bit of sleep', and I hear my father calling and a sigh as she puts the receiver down on the table. I hang up. But I don't know when she does. I hang up but I suspect the line is open all night.

I dream about wetting the bed and after the water goes cold I wake up and find myself in the dry.

'There's no point blaming me,' says Stephen.

So I blame my mother. I blame her because that is what mothers are for. I blame her for the wig and for middle age, for the small corpses she hid behind the sofa and in the wardrobes. Which is to exaggerate, of course. Which is to exaggerate. My mother loved children and welcomed each of us as we came in the door. Still there is something wrong with all this talk of swimming and of babes that strode in smiling through the wicket gate of her heart.

I was a normal birth. Which means that blood and a hole torn out of your arse is normal. Peekaboo.

No. I was not a normal birth. How could I be? Mine was a slow, angry delivery. My mother held on to me like a pervert. I know, because I was there.

So there I was, three weeks overdue. And there was my mother, frightened of what might come out of her. I felt like I was smothering. I would have held my breath but there was no breath to hold in the little wet tea-bags of my lungs (little bags of desire). My hair was grown, my nails were grown, I scratched myself and graffitied her and it must have been the blood-smell that triggered me to — there is no other way to put it — piss myself.

And so I poisoned my mother, nearly killed my mother, who let me go, astonished, violated and clawing at the anaesthetist. I was shot out in a spasm of disbelief that any child could be so ungrateful. We had reached, you might say, a premature understanding.

And holding on to my heel, says Stephen, as Esau held on to Jacob, was my twin brother, whom I dragged out behind me, dead.

'No,' I say.

'Why not?'

'Too easy,' I say. 'Too like original sin', even though as a foetus, you would never call me polite.

'So what am I doing here?' says Stephen.

'I don't know.'

'And what about your mother?' he says. 'Why you were never enough for her, with your seven hundred eyelashes, all your toes and too many teeth.'

But I know my twin, who also had hair, who also had

a tooth. I know how he stayed where he was, even as she let me go. I know how she hoarded him without knowing, how he grew in the dark until they dug him out and put him in a jar. The size of a heart.

I feel my eyeballs start to swell, and it occurs to me, that maybe I cried instead. Maybe it was my tears that bucked her womb and let me go. Maybe I cried with my overdue, opaque child's eyes, saddened her from the inside out, slid into the world oiled with regret. Because I am crying now.

★

'It's not my fault,' she says. 'You only remember the bad things.'

I look at the photograph. My mother is beautiful. She is in love. She looks like the sort of mother you are supposed to remember. It looks like the picture you grow up with. My mother was beautiful and laughing and kind. I cannot fit it inside my head.

I do not remember my mother, how beautiful she was, or how plain. None of us do. She is not that kind of woman. We are not that kind of family. The photo is a lie.

Downstairs, she slices and splits an avocado, squeezes one half to loosen the stone, then slides the skin off intact, with the back of a spoon. She is easy with food, as a mother should be, but the mad-looking green of the avocado makes her hands look old. The other half comes away with a surprising, gritty sound and my mother leaves the empty skin on the table, rocking slightly, like a little coracle holding the stone.

'You sound a little better,' she says.

It is difficult to be angry with an avocado, but I make the effort. It is fairly annoying, sitting there, with the easy significance my mother gives to things, that I cannot figure out — whether it is the way it lies in two halves, or the hole in the middle. Maybe it is the emptiness of the skin or the smooth size of the stone, or the way one sits inside the other, both tear-shaped, both opposite and the same. Or maybe it is that my mother does not care. She has always had this ability just to be.

'He is sleeping a lot,' she says. 'He seems to be sleeping all the time.'

'Really?'

'He is making it up the stairs again.'

'Oh good.'

I go up for a bath though I don't trust the water here either. I pass the pictures on the way and nod at us when we were young. My father must have seen them by now. I feel sorry for him. Maybe he has forgotten himself and thinks it is someone else, up there on the wall.

In the bath I look at the ceiling and at the thin crack in the plaster that has opened its way through successive layers of paint. Its shape, every known wander and divide is known to a part of me that I myself have forgotten. My body changed and grew in this bath. I feel hopeful again and when I get out to dry myself I am too big for the room.

The water runs out quite slowly. There are hairs in the plug hole. Even though they are family hairs, I do not take them out. They are long and grey.

My mother dyes her hair a polite sandy colour that is kind to her face. The colour is real enough. It may not be the colour of real hair, but it is the colour of a real woman's hair, once she has reached a certain age. My mother also keeps a clean house. These are my father's hairs in the plug hole and she has let them be.

I realise that I never really thought about what was under my father's wig. His head, for all I knew, might have been bright green.

Perhaps I thought his baldness was unhealthy, that the hair was just giving up and jumping in patches off his scalp. I was wrong. His hair hung on and grew, helplessly over the years. He must have cut it himself, badly, by touch. He must have swept up after himself, taken strands out of the bath, burnt them perhaps. Now he is sick, my mother pretends that they are not there.

Under his wig, my father is grey. It is a moving colour. I thought these hidden hairs might be the same vicious brown as the ones he wore on the outside; but they grew in the dark, turned silver in the dark. I lift one out to have a look and it curls as it hits the air. It is fine and wet and clings to my finger. I shake my hand and it sticks to my leg. I shake my leg. I hit my thigh. The hair sticks to the base of my thumb before, mercifully, falling to the ground.

As it falls I remember my father with his head jammed in under the sink, newspaper on the lino and the U-bend on the floor. He was probing the pipe, vigorously and precisely, with a wire clothes hanger. There was the sound of ripping from the pipe, a dreadful sound. It reminded me of fake violence on the television, how tough the body really is, how hard to tear. Out of the pipe came a clot of hair which he wiped off on to a piece of newspaper folded around the tip of the hanger. The smell was the only smell that my childhood revolted against. Most other smells, I quite enjoyed.

Like the First Time, Every Time

On the night before the show Stephen is in the final, incandescent stages of paranoia. Everything circles around him before disappearing into his head. His eyes are unbearably bright. I am afraid they will implode.

'All set?' I say.

'Set?'

'What's wrong with you?' I say. 'What are you scared of?'

He shows me the list.

> ballistophobia BULLETS
> eisoptrophobia MIRRORS
> chrometophobia MONEY
> dermatosiophobia SKIN
> pteronophobia FEATHERS
> gephyrophobia BRIDGES

barophobia GRAVITY
onomatophobia NAMES
uranophobia HEAVEN
phagophobia SWALLOWING
hamartophobia SIN
sophobia YOU

I go around the house and in an old and final gesture take all the mirrors off the walls. There is however little I can do about gravity.

I can only get him to bed by bringing the television upstairs. He stops singing to watch but when I turn the sound off he starts to hum along with the pictures. He hums, not easily in the back of his throat where a hum usually sits, but at the front of his mouth, like a sound trying to climb out of his face.

'So tell me something,' I say, wishing instead to touch him as a friend might, a difficult thing to do in a bed.

'Like what?' he says.

'Something you know.'

'Tum Tum,' he says, 'is the talmudic word for an angel whose sex cannot be easily determined.'

'That's a good word.' I thought he might be trying to tell me something. 'Tum Tum.'

'How can they tell?' he says. 'They only knew about two sexes. And women can't be angels.'

'So?'

'So it doesn't matter what you know.'

The news is finishing up on the television. I try to figure out the weather for tomorrow. I cannot go to sleep.

The copulating angels are back, all two hundred of them. The air is full, as they say, with the beating of wings. Mayflies are crawling out of a hole by the tap of the radiator, wet and mutilated. Their wings dry in the heat and make a fierce, inorganic clatter as they take off around the room. Horseflies with florescent eyes for heads extract themselves from the wet tea-leaves in the bottom of a cup. 'Tinkerbell it ain't,' I say and know by my tone of voice that this is a dream, as the maggots do their thing.

Then the birds, all in a flap. Birds with human heads or birds with fat legs and coy little toes. Some of the thrushes have bollocks for their undercarriage and a finch is circling on the concrete, flapping two thin white arms.

A heron stands on the table, stretches like a dinosaur and weeps. On the naked underside of its wings the feathers have rooted up under the transparent skin, like a shoal of sharp-nosed fish, suiciding into a swimmer.

Then the roof clears to sky.

I am woken by his hand leaving my stomach. His hair and his breath are touching my shoulder. His instep pushes quietly up into the arch of my foot.

I feel like someone had told me a joke two months ago and only just remembered the punchline.

The light from the television is shifting and changing at the end of the bed. His body is curved, like the arc of a D against my quiet I. Other than that, the only thing I can think about is the gap between us and about the tip of his tongue, through his open teeth, touching the air of the room.

My body seems to have forgotten what to do with it all, has forgotten how to cross space, how to complete the surprise. My body is still all in bits, and all different ages, so his breath smells like the air outside a dance-hall when you are fourteen years of age, the sheet between us is aching like sixteen, the place where his fingers left my stomach feels hot and twenty-two, and his foot feels old.

He knows I am awake. The distance between us is so simple and white, that I can feel the slither of the sheets as his hand slips through them, stumbles at my hip bone, gathers blindly to find my belly again, where it rests, without moving. We lie there for a while, a difficult H. Waiting.

His tongue tasted so sweet I nearly did not know what it was. The alphabet abandons me as his hand reaches the top of my legs, which quite simply separate as I change from I to Y, though upside down. The words garble in my head, though what followed was not the liquid amnesia of the movies, but fierce and easy and tasting of several different types of skin. The cool baby skin that fitted at the back of his ear, the hot plump skin of his earlobe, the thick but hairless skin of his throat, then the startling velum of his glans, too fine to be called skin at all, the friendly hide of his belly and the complicated and salty crease of his eye, tasting of sleep.

So although I had no words for how new it was, I saw

it all and remembered it all. At least I remember it in bits, how solid his chest was as it gave under the weight of my hand, the awful lightness of his fingers, the light of his eye, the surprising weight of his head, the weightlessness of his mouth, how substantial he was outside of me, though inside there was no end to him.

I came all over the place, as was only to be expected. So it was some time before I worried for him, for the sweat, for the gathering lightness and the fear on his face. I worried for him as he slipped into the helpless and surprising centre of himself, the air over his shoulders fluttering in agitation and his eyes on mine. I did not know what might happen. I thought he might die or weep or disappear. I did not stop it.

I felt it first, a tidal bore, running with unexpected slowness into the very heart of me. A kind of bark from Stephen. Then silence. For the first time since he touched me, I felt frightened. That last wave of his was still going through me. I don't think it stopped. I think it is going through me now.

★

He is cheerful in the morning and sane. I can't believe it was that simple. The sound of the bath water running, the smell of toast and Stephen talking to the toaster saying 'I'm afraid you're going to have to give it up now. I'm afraid you're going to have HUP! Sorry about that.'

I wonder if my body might be blank as a sheet, but in the bath I am all there, soft and tough, blood and bone, each breast jealous of the other and the kisses it remembers. There is a hopeful glow of pink fighting back through the white where Stephen left his mark.

We are shy in the kitchen. I wonder if I might be pregnant. He looks at me in the way you might look at a woman who is pregnant.

We drive into work, while my body secretly remembers all the lettermaking on the white sheets. M was one of them, a touching O, an informal kind of R, for Rumple or embRace, a hilarious K which was just too complicated.

Most of the words made no sense. KORMA for example. There was also DATA, a more reciprocal DATTA, and a very fine HAT of which the T was so distinctive I fell out of the bed. All this as we drive into work — that was another one, with a hip-popping W and an R where Stephen cried. Oh he cried.

He cried. So I made love to him carefully; using my hands carefully to remind him where his body was and where it stopped, to remind him where it stopped and where it turned into something else. Because he was so substantial outside of me but inside there was no end to him. There was no end to him and no telling so I just lost it instead and nearly crashed the car.

'Watch it,' says Stephen. He seems solid enough now. He seems fine. I would have said he was a new man, if I could be sure that man was the right word. He talks to me about buildings we pass, wonders what an office block would look like if the glass just melted, if the carpets started growing, if the phones started ringing like Angelus bells.

'No tricks,' I say.

'Sorry?'

'Just. When we get there. When we hit air. No tricks.'

'Who me?'

'Promise.'

He leans over and kisses me until the lights go green. The shock of his mouth is like everything we did last night all at once. If this is his promise I believe him, though in retrospect, and I have had quite a bit of retrospect, the lights stayed red for an unnaturally long time.

The Colour of Skin

These days I have plenty of time to think. I swim every morning in the sea and pull myself through the ebb of the wave, because the sea is hungry and wants me back. The sea is heavy. I feel the suck of the wave in the morning and water seduces me all day, because it is something to lie on. Water that makes you spread just to look at it, that wants you, small as you are. I cannot find the edge of myself, which is why I have to be inside things now, so that the walls will hold me in, so that I can lap into corners and seep into carpets and carry like a bowl the noise of the sea.

I have plenty of time to tease it apart and fit it together again, what happened on the show and where Stephen went. I have spoken to everyone concerned. I tie it all together and then I cut the string.

Last night I dreamed that Stephen was dead, and that he came into my dream to tell me that he was dead and to tell me something else, which I can't remember. I should not have been surprised. These are things that I already know, in a way.

The Stephen in my dream was the same, though his eyes were larger. His eyes were larger but still the same colour, or so the dream told me.

When I woke it was with the grief of everyone who has ever seen a dead friend in their dreams; the same want; the same ache to sleep again; the same need to hear what they were saying, or about to say, the memory of which is spread through all of you, but gently, like water, like something you cannot pick up.

And the joy that he was there and that he was real. All the dead, they smile or sit or lean forward in just that way. They sit in a way that you had forgotten and lean forward in a real way, just to remind you they are not a dream. 'Yes. It's me.'

They lean forward to tell you what they have come to say and they let you look in to their eyes, which are larger than they used to be, but still the same colour.

You want to see them again but you don't want to die. You just want to sleep again, to be in that place again, where the dead and the living can talk to each other and look into each other's eyes.

I woke up grateful and sick with grief, as if I could not carry my heart anymore; it had burst and spread, like an old yolk.

So I pick up the clues again, as if they mattered. I remember the blur when we arrived in the office, the residue of the night before, or the excitement of going live. Whatever I focused on was simple enough; Frank being calm, Jo being calm, but the LoveWagon was hovering on the edges and every time I looked away from him, Marcus seemed to smile.

I remember Stephen coming to sit with us; with my colleagues, none of whom slept with him the night before, and with me, who did.

He talked to Jo. He talked to Jo as if I wasn't there. He took her stopwatch and handled it, clicked it on — let it run — reset — let it run. His hands looked like a builder's hands. I remember the awful dryness of his palm last night, the lines deepening in the creases, even as I looked at them.

He wraps the stopwatch in its thong and gives it back, still ticking, to Jo, who switches it off casually, as if she didn't know. The year they added an extra second to the clock Jo was the woman up in the studio gallery, counting down for the nation.

'So where did you put the extra second?' Stephen asks. Did she have the old midnight and then a new one a second later? Or did she scrub the old one and just go for the new? Did she say zero twice, and if so which was the right zero? If both were right, what would you call the time in between the two?

Jo smiles and seems to know what he means. He smiles back, as if to thank her for giving us all a little extra time.

Michelle in make-up had never seen such beautiful skin. She looks at him for a while, then looks at him again.

'I'd leave you as you are,' she says, 'except you wouldn't be able to go on without', and Stephen smiles like a cat.

'Slap it on,' he says. 'You need a thick skin for this show.'

So she picks up some foundation with regret, then puts it back down again, picks up a different one, mixes a little in her hand and as he closes his eyes, sponges slowly under his chin and in thick even strokes down his neck. He opens one eye as she works on his face. It worries her, this perfect skin.

'I'll be in to you later to see how you look under the lights.'

She says it firmly, as if the camera would never intervene, as if the guys in Master Control didn't tweak the colour after the man at the lighting desk tweaked the colour after the guys in Maintenance set the colour on the cameras, and all of them with graphs that go up and down to tell them what colour skin is, somewhere between this wavelength and that wavelength of blue or green or red. So they stand back and fix it there — where skin is just honest to God skin, and red is the red they like, the red on the inside of their heads; Manchester United red, blood red or the red they see when they kiss in the dark. Then everyone at home starts fiddling with their own set as if to say, to each man his own kiss. She says it with conviction, as if the sum of all those tweaks and shifts made it true, a kind of skin by consent.

How do you make a decision about colour in that kind of environment? How do you make a decision about red if you have forty shades there set out in a row in front of you, from Burnt Rose to Burgundy to Flame and every single one of them not quite right?

'It's a question of tones, isn't it?' said Stephen and she seems relieved. 'Did you ever work in black and white?'

That is how I remember him, the air blurring around him as his body settled on his bones; as pores opened and age crept in. I should not blame myself. I don't even know what happened when the cameras switched on and he walked into the propellors; when his flesh hit the airwaves. I think he put up a fight anyway. Because, it would seem, we all saw our own show. And here is the best that I can do.

Rehearsal

Edel arrives at 4.15. She is already early. She gets a little bit earlier all the time. She is worried that some day she will meet herself coming back. But the woman at reception isn't surprised.

'Certainly,' she says. 'They'll have someone over right now.'

★

Over in the office they are running late. Frank is putting in some last minute changes. Jo tries not to care, but she follows them all the same.

'The script has already gone to printing,' she says. Frank doesn't hear. He puts his hand over his back pocket and freezes. His wallet, his pictures are gone.

★

A man comes into the reception area and asks her her

name. When she tells him he says 'That's great', as though she had a great name.

'Follow me,' he says and walks through a door. She looks over at the woman behind the reception desk and the woman smiles at her. The smile is for her, but it is also for the row of television sets on the wall, where a cartoon is showing with a cat and a bird. The cat is walking a telephone wire over to the bird's nest. He has an umbrella in one hand, stretched out for balance.

★

Frank enters the studio through the wide scene-dock door, big enough to fit a plane through. He walks across the floor and looks at the lighting rig which creaks and blinks, as one lamp descends on a telescopic hoist. The lamp turns around to look at him with a whirring hum and switches itself on.

'How'ya,' says Frank.

★

Edel follows the man through the door and finds herself in a corridor. It is surprisingly narrow and busy. She doesn't have time to see it all. A man goes past with a dirty duvet cover knotted at the top like a sack. As he goes past she smells something rancid and does not know whether it comes from the man or from the sack. She looks over her shoulder and she sees the sack move. There is something moving inside the duvet cover and it smells.

Marcus is editing the interview from last week's date. The girl on the tape is saying 'Lovely eyes, big smile, really good pectorals, but the best bit is . . . well you know . . . all girls really . . . but me now . . . I really go for . . .'

'Say it,' says Marcus, under his breath. 'Say it.'

'I'm a . . .'

'You're an . . .'

'I like . . .'

'You like a nice . . .'

'I like a nice . . .'

'arse.'

'personality.'

'What?' said Marcus. 'That's not what she said this morning.'

'Women,' said the editor. 'Always changing their minds.'

★

The man brings her down the corridor and around the corner where someone is shouting 'Run. Run now.' A woman turns around and collides with her and five tapes land on the ground, their cases burst open, one of them goes skittering across the carpet and hits the wall. Edel bends down to pick them up.

'Sorry,' she says and the two women's heads bang off each other. The woman who was holding the tapes doesn't say anything to her, she says 'Oh Jesus. Oh Jesus.'

★

Up in the box Frank dials a number and says 'What's the story on Camera 3? We are going live in three hours' time. What do you want me to do? Cut to black?' and his wife's voice says 'Frank? Who gave you my number? Is this a joke?'

★

She follows the man through a door and into make-up.

'This is Edel', he says, 'for the LoveQuiz.'

'How are you?' says a woman in make-up. 'Take a seat.' She climbs up into what looks like a barber's chair, the woman takes a pink bib, snaps it into the air, twists the top around her neck and lets the rest drift down onto her chest.

'Nervous?' says the woman.

'No,' says Edel. 'I mean yes.' She looks down at her knee and sees a ladder in her tights, running up under her skirt, even as she watches it.

★

'When I saw her first . . . Ready? OK. When I saw her first I thought Nice face, Shame about the dress. No. No. The first thing I saw were her eyes which are green, a really witchy, seductive green. Brown. Let me try that again. When I saw her first I thought Hello . . . We're going to have a good time.'

★

Stephen waves at the camera, just like he is told and the

light around his head separates out into red and green and blue.

★

The man sitting in the next chair to Edel gives her a wink. She thinks it might be the Minister for Health and Social Welfare.

'Mmmmnn,' says the Minister. He closes his eyes. 'That's lovely,' he says. 'You know there's nothing so lovely as being made-up.' The make-up woman leans across him. Her breast touches his ear.

★

'Stand by for rehearsal,' says Frank. 'In five. Get wardrobe to do something with that guy's white shirt — it's flaring all over the place. Cue Damien. Cut two. *What?*'

All the screens have gone to white.

★

Stephen looks up and sees me on the gantry, looking down. He seems scared. He smiles anyway. Pop goes a light, showering the floor with sparks and glass. Bang goes my heart. Pop goes my breast.

And at last I know the difference between one and two.

'One. *Tchuu*,' says Stephen into the mike. 'One. *Tchew.*'

★   ★

Frank leaves the studio while they fix the cameras and he goes to the toilet. There is a smell in the next cubicle and a man is making a noise in there. It sounds like he is feeding hens, or a calf. He is making wet clucking sounds deep in his throat. Frank hears the toilet flush and the man say 'Oh no you don't.'

★ ★

Maybe he isn't the Minister for Health and Social Welfare. Edel notices that he is sliding his hand up and down the back of the make-up lady's knee. Every stroke of his hand goes a little further up her skirt.

★ ★

'Well let's eat in the hotel,' I said. 'If you want me to wear a dress.' I just thought he didn't like my legs. That said I thought well here's a lovely person, kind eyes and a good listener, maybe it was because his mouth was always full. No I didn't say that. Don't put that in.'

'Leave it in,' says Marcus.

★ ★

The Head of Current Affairs comes into the toilet and goes up to the urinal. Frank edges away from the cubicles. His back brushes the back of the Head of Current Affairs, who looks over his shoulder. Frank catches his eye. They listen. There is the sound of the piss of the Head of Current Affairs hitting the urinal and, from the cubicle, the sound of a man saying 'Come on. Come on you little sweetheart, you little bastard. Come on.'

The make-up woman is leaning across the Minister for Health and Social Welfare. She is patting his face with a soft, dry, firm powder puff. He is stroking the top inside of her thigh. She says 'How's that now?'

'Lovely,' he says and opens his eyes. 'Just lovely.' She smiles down at him.

★ ★

'Great kisser. I mean classic kisser. And he says "Listen, come on" because I wasn't really interested to tell you the truth but he was really hot to trot. Talk about Russian hands, talk about Roman fingers! Anyway. It was a beautiful night. Very warm. And "Fuck you" he's saying.'

'Out on "fingers",' says Marcus.

★ ★

The only sound in the toilet is the sound of the piss of the Head of Current Affairs and the sound of the man inside the cubicle, who is saying 'Eat it, you little bastard. Eat it.' Frank bends down to check how many pairs of shoes are visible under the door. The toilet seat falls with a clatter and the man says 'Damn.' A stained sheet is thrown over the cubicle door and a small white mouse runs from under the partition and across the shoes of the Head of Current Affairs, where it gets very wet.

'Damn,' says the Head of Current Affairs.

$\star$ $\star$

'Just lie back there,' says the woman from make-up.

'Take as long as you like,' says the Minister for Health and Social Welfare.

'I'll just neaten you up a little,' she says, taking up her tweezers. 'You know what they say about men', she says, 'whose eyebrows meet.'

$\star$ $\star$

'I've never seen anything like it,' says the camera-man to Frank. 'The pictures are back, they're just coming in upside down.'

'Well stand on your head, why don't you,' says Frank.

$\star$ $\star$

'This big prick with a vein in it and I'm saying Just please let me go to the toilet, I have to go to the toilet, I'll be back in a minute I swear, I swear and he just says nothing and I can't move and this big ignorant looking prick pushing.'

'Rewind,' says Marcus.

$\star$ $\star$

'Aaargh!' says the Minister, as the woman from make-up examines the tuft of hair in her tweezers. His body stiffens in the chair, his hand under her skirt makes a fist.

'You BITCH!' he screams and the Special Branch man runs into the room with a gun in his hand.

Jo checks her stopwatch and her stand-by stopwatch counts up her durations. Then she checks them again. One of her stopwatches is out.

★   ★

There is a scream from make-up. The Special Branch man drops his sandwich. It takes him three long seconds to get his gun out of the holster. The screaming has stopped. He bursts in through the door and covers the room. The gun goes off. A mirror shatters and Edel's face falls on the counter. .

★   ★

'Physically,' says Frank. 'Turn the camera physically upside down.' A pair of feet walks across the ceiling, top of the frame, then spins around and walks across the floor.

★   ★

'Great kisser I mean a really classic kisser and he says "Listen, come on" because I wasn't really interested to tell you the truth, but he was really hot to trot. Talk about Russian hands, talk about Roman fingers! Anyway it was a beautiful night. Really warm, "Fuck this" he says. "Let's go for a swim" he says, "Everyone's asleep. We might be the only two people left in the world." '

'What?' says Marcus.

★   ★

Jo has synchronised her watches. She puts her hand on
Frank's arm.

*   *

'Nobody move,' says the Special Branch man. 'Or I'll
take out my gun.' There is a man at the back of the room
holding a stained sheet. He's saying 'Come on. Come on.'
The Special Branch man looks at the floor, where a snake
is winding its way around the base of one of the chairs.
It is heading this way.

'It's only a snake,' says the man. 'I can't leave it in my
dressing room.' The Special Branch man is afraid of snakes.

*   *

I arrive in make-up and Michelle sort of glares at me and
indicates with her eyes where the guy is sitting with his
snake. Every one is being very professional.

'David, is it?' I say and shake his hand. 'What are you
up here for? Giving Patrick a lick of Vaseline?' Patrick is
the snake.

*   *

And that is all before we hit air. Stephen blamed Patrick,
but he would, wouldn't he. He would blame the snake.

I go up to hospitality.

'So Edel,' I say, 'all set?'

'I have a ladder in my tights,' she says.

The television is on in the corner. She has switched over to Countdown where Carol is doing a numbers quiz.

'She's amazing with numbers,' I say, for the sake of it.

'Why is she always pregnant?' says Edel. 'I mean, when is she due?' And it is true that every time you see her, Carol from Countdown is still pregnant. She has been about seven months gone all year.

'They record them all together,' I say. 'They record about twenty shows in a week and then put them out one at a time.'

'Oh right,' says Edel. But she is not convinced. She looks at Carol like there was one thing she could not count and that was the days left, as if all the numbers in her head had knocked a few out of her belly. And we both look at her bump, where that baby sits from month to month, on the telly, just as happy as it ever was. Resisting time.

Steady as She Go-Goes

So Camera 3 is still upside down everybody and we're WINGING IT. As directed.

Fifteen seconds to air.

So Plan B. Coming out on the topshot on 4 followed by the wide on 3. Sorry my mistake.

Wide on 2. Wide on 2. Check?

Check. Check.

Single on 1, applause on 4.

One here. I've just gone upside down Frank.

I saw that. I saw that. So Plan C. Topshot on 4. Wide on 2 pan right for Damien, track in to head and shoulders. You're on your own Mick. Check?

Check. Check.

Ten seconds to opening animation. Studio two to Pres. Stand by Basketweaving Documentary.

Two cameras down. Get one back and we can make it.

Eh Frank

Yes I saw that. I see that. Camera 2 has just flipped. We are falling off the air.

Seven seconds. Six. Roll both VTs.

We are going down.

VTs Rolling. Opening on VT1 and Basketweaving on VT2.

Please make sure your tray table is in an upright position. Or No. We can flip the output. Just the output. FLIP THE OUTPUT! Yes. We have three cameras. We're on our way. *Coming to VT!*

And take it! Coming out of the opening animation to 3 on the wide, then MCU on 2 of the fat bastard. Sorry. Plan for Camera 1, applause shots and wide, then singles guys during game.

Twenty seconds to studio.

Camera 2 single Damien and wide Damien–plus–game. Camera 3 on the singles/two shots guys. I know it's upside down for you, but it's coming out clean at the other end.

Camera 4 has just flipped. Ten seconds to studio.

I saw that. Back on script. We hit lucky. We're back on script.

Five seconds to studio.

Coming out of this to four. Back on script.

Three.

Two.

One.

Go Grams. Cut

Zero.

Four.

LADIES AND GENTLEMEN

Good luck everyone.

IT'S THE LOVEQUIZ!

Applause applause. Coming to single on 2. Cue Damien.
Cut 2.

★ ★

At home my mother settles in to do her duty and pretend
to watch the LoveQuiz. My father is sleeping, as usual, in
his chair. During the ads he looks like he is having a bad
dream. When the LoveQuiz music comes on he wakes up
and looks at the set in surprise. He says:
  'Where's the baskets.'
  'It's Grainne's programme,' says my mother. 'Look.'
  'Where are the baskets,' says my father. He is upset.
  'No baskets,' says my mother.
  'Baskets!' he is shouting.
  'It's the television,' she says. 'It was just a dream.'
  When Damien appears on the screen my father grabs his
head and shouts.
  'Bastards.'
  'Basket or bastards. Make up your mind,' says my mother.
  'I know what I'm saying,' he says.
  She believes him.
  'It's upside-down,' he says.

★ ★

The cameramen float around behind the peds with cricks
in their necks. They can't frame up properly, the lenses
keep drifting towards people's feet. For a while they check
around the side of the cameras to see what is for real. Then
they forget real because it is less confusing that way.

200

In the gallery all the monitors are showing upside down except for the transmission picture. Jo refuses to see, she just looks at the script, at her watch, at people on the screens, and she reads it like it is. Frank looks like he is in a dream. Not a bad dream.

★   ★

'So it's a new game for the biggest the best the last show of the season. Out of these five contestants, only three make it to round two. But do they go home empty handed? Or do they wander off with a wad of wonga? It depends on how much they put on that table to woo the woman of their dreams when it's time to . . . all together . . . *put your money where your mouth is!* Thank you. So the lady decides and the fella who gets her, gets half the money on the table — as well as the sneaky stash he hid in his back pocket.

'So let's have a look at de loverly lady who's going to pick de lucky fella. Shush! Here she comes . . . The most beautiful woman in Dublin 14 — who laughed? — no seriously, she's as sweet and gorgeous as you could meet. May I introduce you to Edel from Rathfarnham!!'

★   ★

In short, the show was fine. An unusual number of technical difficulties were reported but no pattern was established. Faults logged included:

bleeding: Mayo

tearing: Clones

break-up: Cork

vertical hold: Armagh
horizontal hold: Dundrum
strobing: Nobber
double image: Glenageary
after image: Timoleague
flare/streaking — from Kilkee to Newbliss
cramping/stretching/bending of the picture — general
snow — also general

Seventeen people rang in to say that Damien's flies were open, which I must say I never noticed. My mother thought the laugh track was a great addition, until she realised that it was leaking in from another channel. She realised this when people persisted in laughing at the wrong things.

The boys played the games. Eddie, Kevin, Sean, Jake and Stephen raced across ropes and mud, to reach a bouquet of flowers, a voucher for a washing machine, a necklace, a collection of silk underwear, or a snake. There was some confusion over the snake. It ended up in the mud and wrapped itself around Stephen's right leg. He wrestled with the snake and dropped the flowers into the mud. Damien came in to pull the snake off his leg and five people rang in to complain on behalf of the snake, the sixth person said that he was Charles II and knew what we were up to there in Dublin 4 with the niggers and the Jews.

Later, inside the station it was reported that the LoveWagon was seen snogging with the Minister for Health and Social Welfare, until he turned out to be the Minister for something else. This was after he wandered on to the set by accident.

'Who's that?' said Frank.

'Looks like some politician,' said Jo.

'Cue applause. Cut one. We'll take a break,' says Frank. 'Please get the politician off the set.'

The LoveWagon was also reported crying in the carpark, laughing in hospitality, drunk in the scene dock, on the ball in Master Control. Rumour had her licking the sound man's ear, eyeing a cameraman, cutting the editor down to size and giving a stage-hand some manual relief. But as far as I could see, she spent the evening talking to Marcus in an undertone getting her jokes laughed at.

Inside the LoveBox, Edel was sitting out the games, with a pair of headphones on, through which she listened to 10cc's Greatest Hits. At home my father sang along.

The LoveBox has no roof. When Edel looked up at the gantry she saw a woman looking down at her. It was me. We waved.

Inside the Big Blow the fellas waited for the wind machine and for the trapdoor to release all those twenty pound notes. Eddie grabbed twenty-six of them, Kevin got twenty-one, Sean got seven, Jake got seventeen and Stephen got one.

'OK,' said Damien. 'It's time to *Put your money where your mouth is!* and remember you guys — the fella who wins the girl also gets half the money on the table — so are you going to risk it? Or will you sneak some into your back pocket? — she'll never know.'

PLAYER	ON THE TABLE	IN HIS BACK POCKET	AUDIENCE REACTION
EDDIE	Snake + £360	£160	**BOO**
KEVIN	Silk Underwear + £420	nothing	**CHEER**
SEAN	Necklace + £140	nothing	**AWWWW**
JAKE	Washing Machine +£140	£200	**MIXED**

STEPHEN put one broken lily on the table with the single £20 he had managed to catch. The audience went **AWWWW**. Then he reached into his back pocket and hauled out £57.75 in fives and tens and coins. He put it on the table. The audience went **WILD**. I assume he stole the money from me over the past few months, unless he stole it from someone else.

'And now,' says Damien, 'if that wasn't soppy enough, it's time to get your LovePens out, remember it's a two-line poem, it's for Edel and it's about LOVE, and while you're doing that, we'll go to a commercial break.'

The ads were as follows:

An antiperspirant ad set in a jungle
A car ad set in a desert
A butter ad set in the family home
A toilet paper ad set in the family home
A chocolate ad showing chocolate

None of them was the wrong way around. The car ad was not set in the family home, it was free of references to butter. There was no toilet paper in the jungle or antiperspirant in the car. There was no chocolate in the ad for toilet paper. The chocolate stayed in the chocolate ad and avoided the family home. The desert was beautiful. I was beginning to relax. At home, my father went up to the bathroom and did not come down for some time.

The LovePoems were as follows:

EDDIE (snake

    + £360)   I'm going to slither up and squeeze you
                  And hiss while I kiss and tease you
                  Please? Let me please you.

KEVIN (underwear

    + £420)   Satin and lace. Your lovely face
                  All I can say is 'Back to my place?'

SEAN (necklace

    + £140)   True heart, good as gold
                  Love can't be bought and it can't be sold

JAKE (washing machine

    + £140)   I'm not very good at rhyme and there
                        isn't a lot of time
                  To say how I feel — Let's make it real.

STEPHEN (lily

    + £77.75)   I will not let you go.

'Is that it?' said Damien.

'That's it,' said Stephen. The slut. The boys are sent behind their screen.

Edel steps out of the LoveBox and her headphones are removed. She blinks slightly at the light. Through the sudden glare, she sees herself in a monitor and smiles. She looks at the table. I can tell that she really wants the washing-machine but I can also tell that she will not choose it. She picks the silk underwear + £450. Then she takes the snake for a laugh, and maybe for the money. She hesitates between the necklace and the flower for simplicity of heart, then goes for the flower because it is more dangerous.

'Perfect,' says Damien as the snake slips away, only to be caught on Camera 3, which has slid inevitably down to the floor again. And everyone screams.

The next set of ads had a butter ad showing butter, a car ad set mid air, a famine relief ad set in the desert, and a chocolate ad set in the family home which turns into the jungle when a man falls through a bookcase.

After the break Damien introduces last week's lucky couple who sit on the sofa, holding hands. They listen to what they said about each other in the interview and they laugh. My father shouts 'Prick!' He shouts 'Get out of the pool!' — but you probably have got the picture by now.

Marcus looks at the interview with a feeling in his heart that he will not remember. The LoveWagon says 'Brilliant.' He looks at her and does not know what she means.

'What do you mean?' he says.

'The best this season. For tatty sex and the helpless heart.'

My father pokes the television set with his stick and flicks over to a political debate on the other side, where they are discussing abortion or artificial insemination or in vitro fertilisation or condoms or foetuses in the cosmetics industry or brain dead mothers or gender abortions or infanticide as so often happens in Studio 4, when the snake makes its appearance, causing a lot of discomfort to the Minister, who has begun to feel that it is not his evening.

'It is a snake,' he says. The presenter keeps his cool and attacks.

'A snake? That has been banished from our shores? Is that what you are saying? Minister?'

Afterwards the presenter says that he did not even notice the animal under the table. He says that live television has the same effect on your heart rate as going into combat and he has done it four hundred and seventy-five times. He says he should be dead. We give him a large whiskey and make jokes about purple hearts.

My father flicks back for the end of the show.

'It's all wrong,' he says. 'It's all upside down.' So he goes into the corner of the room and stands on his head. The names my mother uses to try to get him to stop include 'Sweetheart', 'Dear', 'Sweetheart' again and 'Love'. She also calls him by his own, given name, which none of us have heard in a long time.

'Remember me?' he says. 'Remember me like this?'

'Come on now love,' she says, but he stays as he is.

Edel asks each of the three guys a question.

Edel to Sean: If we were all alone in the garden would you be a snake in the grass?
Sean to Edel: I'd be the apple of your eye. I would charm the fig leaf off you.

Edel to Kevin: Satin and lace is all very well, but what would *you* wear on that special date?
Kevin to Edel: My heart on my sleeve.

Edel to Stephen: Thanks for the flower.
Stephen to Edel: It's all yours.
Edel: It's a bit smashed.
Stephen: But it's all yours. Because television has no smell.

A set blew up in Templeogue. But the transmission masts stood firm, took the signal and sent it on. Though snow was reported falling on Kippure, a light was seen on Mount Leinster and up around Three Rock, the sheep went mad. The signal took its own time, as fast as now is, as slow as the present. It shot along the link to Cairn Hill, to Truskmore and Maghera, snaked up to the tip and was hurled into the wide blue. It was caught in Achill and Kilkeaveragh, on Mount Gabriel and Holywell Hill, patted on the head and thrown further on. Fifty times a second it did this, in alternate scans, two half pictures meshing into one so you couldn't tell the difference, and the televisions in Kiltemagh and Gowra, in Newry and Inch glowed red and green and